Kram, Mark
Miles to go

MILES TO GO

MILES
TO GO

by
MARK KRAM

WILLIAM MORROW AND COMPANY, INC.

New York   1982

Library of Congress Cataloging in Publication Data

Kram, Mark.
  Miles to go.
  I. Title.
PS3561.R24M5   813.54   81-11264
ISBN 0-688-00451-2   AACR2

Printed in the United States of America
First Edition
1 2 3 4 5 6 7 8 9 10

To the members of the Todds Road Stumblers, Lexington, Kentucky, so generous with their time and research. And to Alex Campbell for the idea and tenacious support.

It is horrible, yet fascinating,
this struggle between a set purpose
and an utterly exhausted frame.

—SIR ARTHUR CONAN DOYLE
on seeing Dorando Pietri
collapse three times in
the last hundred yards of
the 1908 Olympics

What is now proved was once only imagined.

—WILLIAM BLAKE

MILES TO GO

1

They flowed out of the ancient square like multicolored grains of sand from an hourglass, out of the center of Addis Ababa, the three-thousand-year-old capital of Ethiopia and the start of the first annual Abebe Bikila Memorial Marathon, 26 miles and 385 yards of the cruelest torture, even for a world-class marathon. Slowly, the field stretched into a mile-long line as it passed centuries of architectural evolution on its way into the lushness of the Great Rift Valley. After the early miles of honking Citroëns and Alfas that snarled by and faded into the dust, after the VW buses loaded with drowsing Belgian tourists, the caravans of pushcarts and ribbons of market stalls, they ran, too briefly, in the early light of autumn morning along silent byways that cut the valley into a patchwork of green and gold and almost amber. And soon the reason for the early start was with them; the furnace heat that was whipping down from the sudden foothills of a mountain range.

Out in front, the American Roy Holt ran over the world-class names in his mind. Knudsen of Norway; one of the lesser Russians; a trio of Kenyans; Militades of Greece; Overbeck of East Germany—the best in the field of four hundred from thirty nations. Having heard some talk earlier in the week, Roy sensed that the champions would be short on desire and try to evade the rack. They were not about to go up against the thin air of Ethiopia (altitude: 7,000 feet), the blazing sun or the terrain to risk injury and ego for what was, they knew, a simple gesture of diplomacy on the part of their nations. Except for Franz Overbeck, thought Roy. The colossus of the marathon, in every facet of his persona and conformation the perfect receptacle for East German science and ambition in athletics, Overbeck never ran an inch without grim intent. Franz Overbeck would be along in a while. And, thought Roy, the East German could have the race; Roy wanted more from this race than victory, that one word that had propelled his whole life. He warned himself not to be drawn into a contest of wills with the East German.

Roy's thoughts turned to Bikila, who had died in 1973. The Ethiopian had always been his kind of runner: smooth, relentless, unencumbered by theory or technique, a natural. Roy had only been a kid when Bikila slid out of the pack at the 1960 Olympic Games, his bare, black feet gliding like a black mamba moving over a series of anthills. Bikila had set the Olympic record that day: two hours, fifteen minutes, sixteen seconds. Four years later in Japan, with shoes on, he did 2:12:11. By 1969, after a car accident, he would never walk again. There were pictures: the stone legs drooping in the wheelchair, and always the lion sitting next to him as a reminder of the little man's former dominance.

❀ ❀ ❀

Roy squinted an eye up at the yellow sky. It had been eighty when the starter's gun filled the air with pigeons six miles back, and now the land that looked so biblically romantic in the blue light seemed ominous and inexorable. His eyes itched and burned as his headband failed to hold the sweat. Figures in the distance, the hill shepherds, where the ill-defined edges of the road seemed to converge, appeared to be dancing on waves of heat and looked like images caught by a gauzed camera lens. Roy had been in many marathons before, from Singapore to Boston, but this hard land seemed to be catching for the first time the essence of the marathon in his mind, offering up the history of the event itself, the kind of history that seemed like water on a chunk of dry, hot stone; it was there and then it was gone.

He could never get a grip on marathon history. It seemed diffuse, bland, defying permanence in his own mind by its centuries of sprawl, lacking the rich, grand teture of baseball, football or boxing. Of course, there were the signposts: the Greek warrior Pheidippides (or was it Phillipides; nobody could agree on the name or the distance he had run) falling over dead after giving his message of Grecian triumph in battle; the 1896 Olympics, when an obscure Greek shepherd named Spiridon Loues ran across the plain of Marathon, saving the day for Greece against the much-hated "professionalism" of America; the gallant Dorando Pietri of Italy, only a quarter of a mile from the finish in the 1908 London Olympics, turning and running in the opposite direction and then finally losing after a good lead, exhausted and crawling toward the finish line.

Holt closed off his musing as a cadence of feet moved up behind him, annoying him because of its suddenness; he had been out front and alone now for nearly ten miles. He didn't look back. He didn't care about his position. Again, he reminded himself that he wasn't there to win. This race was a lab for his body and mind. The clock could only be a distraction. He was here to find out where the stresses were in his will and muscles. Beat the devil here—the Oslo collapse; he had to. He had paid heavily over the past year and a half for a chance at this gauntlet: the bleeding toes, the blisters, the muscles that felt like cold iron, the emptiness that came from having pulled up his roots in a small Ohio town and moving to Manhattan, where nobody knew him or cared a damn about him, where he could reshape himself. Finally, he had entered his first race in a long time. He got the feel of things in Cleveland. Time: two hours, twenty minutes. He improved some in Louisville, then moved on to Atlanta to sharpen his speed. Came Toronto, and he was down to 2:11. And everywhere the crowds—sensing the promise of drama, of public ruin—gaped and waited for Roy Holt to self-destruct again into little pieces.

Behind him, the feet drew closer. For an instant the thick shadow jiggled over his shoulder, and then it was gone. Somebody in back of him wanted to play a stupid mind game.

The hills were a vise of heat. Holt's long legs gathered in the miles. His thoughts turned back to Bikila. The history of the marathon began and ended for Roy with the lithe African. He wondered if the man had ever run this exact course. How had he handled the ruts and rocks of these hills without shoes? He then thought of him being absurdly imprisoned in the space of his wheelchair, when once those legs seemed to carry him through infinity. Roy could see him sitting there looking up at these same hills and thinking about all the miles he would never run again, the dirty irony of having lost the center of his being: his legs. Roy knew what it was to look for that center one day and to come up empty. That was their common bond: a swift nothingness and the finality of no more miles to go. But after today, he thought, he would smash their link of impotence. He would crash through, back to his own center. He would be whole again. There would be no more fear.

The shadow drifted across the rocks until it was now once more over Roy's shoulder.

Franz Overbeck did not have to see the face to know who was in front of him. Every aspect of Holt—the indolent stride, the long legs, the square shoulders—had already formed an impression on his mind, ever since the Montreal Olympics in 1976, when those legs had traveled up his back and through his reputation. Overbeck studied those legs from no more than five feet back. He watched Holt's thin ankles strain to stay vertical as he ran in and out of the deep ruts and last violent rains had gouged in the slopes that rose up so abruptly. He wondered why Holt did not look back. He pulled up next to the American, who still did not turn his head.

"Go on . . . take it," said Roy, looking straight ahead. "I have other things on my mind."

"*Nein*," said Overbeck.

Roy turned his head. The East German was smiling, pointing to Holt and then himself. "No," said Roy, "I don't want to hunt today. You want it . . . take it."

Stay in the lab, thought Roy, don't let Overbeck get inside. There was only one victory he cared about today: the triumph of will over fear. He did not want to spend his energy of mind on the East German in a witless duel of egos, proving nothing except that he could win or lose another

race. The numbers had bored him, had begun to lack meaning even before the devastating Oslo race back in 1981 in
which Holt had almost died. He wanted more for himself
from the marathon; he wanted to take the event beyond the
limitations of current reality. He had muscled the course
and time into almost implausible shape back there, but he
had left Oslo with his psyche split in two like dry timber
and a dread that followed him like another man's shadow.
And now here in this godforsaken land, now, today, he was.
going to lose the shadow or never run again. His plan was
simple: hurl himself hard against the heat, the air, the terrain of Ethiopia and then gun the next six miles with fury.
He would crack or survive to go once more nearer the
edge.

What the hell, he thought, that was what the marathon
was about. If it had any meaning at all—and it did in the
deepest way for him—the marathon meant passion, pitting
yourself against yourself, a senseless abstraction to many
but a vial of life for Roy Holt, and never more so than right
now. He gave up trying to explain it to himself; the world
was too full of lame analysis that crushed everything into
tiny bits of fashionable meaning. The way he felt was the
only meaning. He loved it all: the sweat running down the
backs of his legs; the burning eyes; the pain in his legs; and
most of all the fear slowly seeping from his mind as he con-
quered each ferocious mile.

Franz Overbeck had dropped back twenty yards off the
pace and was now framing Roy in his mind like an old, lost
picture. But this was not the Holt that he had known, the
tough, storied American who had beaten him, the last time
they had met, for the gold medal in the ten thousand meters

in Montreal, then gone on to win twenty-two of twenty-four international marathons, including Boston three times —in '77, '78 and '79. Franz had waited for him in Moscow in '80, but politics kept the Americans away. Now the American would not engage him. He seemed detached, no longer the killer, that goading form of violent blood and gristle that seemed to enjoy running another man into the ground. What had happened to him? This was not the Holt of Oslo, who had set his dramatic world record of two hours and five minutes. After that day, Holt had faded out of sight. There were rumors: Holt was sick; he would never run again. But Holt was here now. There might never be another chance; Overbeck had to spit up the bile of Montreal.

That day, the biggest one of his life—he could see it all so clearly now. And the American had taken it from him. Earlier, Franz had won the five thousand meters, and he was coming around the last turn in the ten thousand: calm, oblivious, his second gold medal so close. He had caught the last split going into the final lap from his trainers, and then suddenly he heard the long sweeping swish and then the great roar from the crowd that seemed to come up from the bottom of the earth. He looked back over his left shoulder; he saw no one. The footsteps kept coming. He looked over his other shoulder just in time to see Roy Holt flying toward him no more than three body lengths off his flank.

The adrenaline had rushed up through him and then died like a sparkler falling into water. Holt had moved up next to him, those long legs beating him a meter every three strides as they kicked toward the tape. The American won the gold, and Overbeck had to live with the certainty of his own ineptness, the glance of disgust back at his East German training camp up in the Harz Mountains. The memory, the sound of the crowd, the slanting sunlight across the track, every detail of the day was locked behind a dark, iron door in Franz Overbeck's mind. He had moved on to the marathon two years later and won twenty-four out of twenty-four races over the years, including the Moscow Olympics; but he could never forget the American Holt. He would make Holt run today, if only because Holt was here and still goading him with his every stride, though Franz was sure he was up against only a leftover man.

Mercifully, the course stopped climbing, and now they were moving on a quarter-mile of goat path with thorn-bushes on one side and a steep embankment on the other, maybe fifty feet deep. Then the course twisted down the side of the mountain into a gulch that was little more than a dry streambed.

The sides seemed to close in on Roy as he fought for his balance. Up ahead, he saw two natives standing next to a single steel oil can, with dippers and cups in their hands. Water. We could use some. He slowed down, his hand reaching out, and Overbeck flew by him. knocking the cup out of his hand. Roy stumbled to his left, and the anger rushed through him before a streak of clarity quelled him: the East German was looking back and laughing. He couldn't let Overbeck get away with a move like that, for sooner or later it would trouble him, because if you were world-class and didn't have pride you didn't have anything at all, and nobody would understand that he had been trying to work on his mind here. All that they would know was that the East German had squashed Roy Holt like a fly in Ethiopia; when Overbeck put it to him, Holt had bailed out.

* * *

The American, thought Overbeck, would be coming at
him soon. By instinct and character, he knew Holt could
never resist a brawl. And now here he was, climbing up his
back, giving him a real victory to take back to Herr Albrecht, head of East Germany's track and field. So it did not
matter whether or not the American's career was in strands.
He was flesh and blood, and he was here and trying to win,
and that was all that counted; Franz didn't want a setup in
any shape.

"Get the hell out of the way!" yelled Roy, peeling out to
the side of the East German. Roy didn't look over at him,
just kept his eyes ahead, the words bobbing in his throat.
"In Montreal. Remember that party? What I said to you?
The best you're ever going to see. You hear me! I'm still
the best!" Overbeck looked at him strangely: the emotion
startled him.

His own words seemed to echo back to Roy. He hadn't
talked that way in years. The words sounded good, like
brilliant and clear notes caught by a trumpet sliding over a
riff. And suddenly the words dug into him, cutting away a
dark and remote abscess in his being that was known only
to him. He kept saying the words over and over to himself,
and for the first time since Oslo he began to feel free of the
terror that had crippled his mind just as surely as that accident had taken away the legs of the great Bikila. But even
now, just the allusion to Oslo sent a neon sign flashing in his
head and a voice coming out of some faraway, vast chamber: *You don't have to win, Roy. Why go on with this?
You don't want the hell of Oslo again.*

Panic rushed up to his head, and he hung for a moment
caught between that soothing, sympathetic chamber voice
and the sting of the East German's cheap water-cup trick,

that calculated assault on his character. Seven more miles to go, and Holt knew they were now moving away from the dark perimeter into the white-hot center that is in every marathon whether in Dubuque or Boston, that twilight zone place where the character and body begin to buckle and the runner—the great and anonymous alike—must make a choice: keep running or quit. *Be reasonable, Roy, you're not here to win, it's only a race*, the voice purred from the chamber again. "Goddamn it, no!" screamed Roy, his anguish ricocheting through the silence and gray rocks. The East German looked back at him from five yards ahead, stunned by the cry that sounded like that of an animal with a bullet in its belly.

They were rattling down the mountain, sliding, trying to hold their footing, the dust swirling about them. By now, they were twenty-two miles into the course, and they could see three miles of grassy plain opening up before them. Roy watched the East German keep a tight grip on his small lead. Overbeck's body was made for this course, thought Roy: short, thick, with the kind of legs that could be used to knock down buildings, and a deep chest that overwhelmed the thin air and let him breathe evenly and smoothly. He was a piece of running beauty, all right, a perfectly tooled and wired machine. Overbeck, too, had gotten much stronger since Montreal. Roy stayed close for the next mile, and then, as they hit the dirt road leading to the plain, he surged to the lead.

Jerking his head to the side, the East German cracked back in front. He was excited now. Had the American been decoying him over all these miles? Holt was now running with a deadly resolve. So much the better, thought Overbeck; beating this kind of effort would wipe away the Montreal incident forever in his mind. Like a man with one last bullet he concentrated on the precise moment and place when he should squeeze off his strength and speed at the American. He didn't want Holt on his back going into the chute. He'd have to waste him on the plains that led into the city.

There was a water station as they came down off the road, and this time Roy grabbed a cup in each hand and sucked all the water into his cottony mouth. He wanted to throw some on his face to cut the dust caked inside his nostrils, to cool his dry, cracking lips. By the time they broke onto the plain, he and Overbeck were nearly dead even. They could see the spires of Addis Ababa, the flagpole outside the town clustered with people, three miles of flat, still grass ahead. Now, thought Roy, we know you're beautiful, but let's see if Franz Overbeck has gotten any tougher since Montreal.

The flagpole drew closer, and they shot down the straightaway side by side until Roy's foot found a rock hidden in the grass. He staggered and bumped against the East German, who swiftly rammed his elbow twice into the American's rib cage. He pushed off Roy with the second elbow jab, sending him into a drunken wobble that helped the East German to a twenty-yard lead by the time he stepped past the flagpole and onto the paved roads that snaked into the city. Overbeck allowed himself one last glance back at the American. He was pleased with the lead he saw. But he knew the rest of the way in would favor the American's long legs. He knew Holt would cut into that lead; but he had to make him fight for every inch and keep him from getting all of it. He must hold on now, though he knew he was coming apart from the heat and sun. He had been too brazen with the land and climate and Holt. Just like that, he thought, and he was near ruin.

Holt riveted his eyes on the veering Overbeck, his number growing larger in the distance. He'll never make it, thought Roy. He's going to crawl into the chute. He didn't feel too good himself. But still, he thought he had enough left to put the East German away. He focused on Overbeck's number, 49, making it grow bigger and bigger until he could get close enough to pull it off. He cut the East German's lead down to ten yards as they started through the congested streets, where the soldiers held back the crowd. The gap dwindled to five yards as they turned the corner and saw the square and the banners and the finishing chute up ahead.

Roy forced his stride open to the limit. He knew he was taking one step to every two of Overbeck's. The East German's lead was shrinking like wet leather in the Ethiopian sun. The machine was listing badly. Roy focused on the chute. There was a band beyond the finish line. He could see the brass instruments glinting in the sunlight. He wanted to put his hands up to his burning eyes. The blurred image of Overbeck was only a couple of arm's lengths away. Some guys never learn, thought Roy. "You're all mine!" yelled Roy. The crowd heard him and roared.

As they hit the chute, their breaths whistling, their skins red and blotched, their legs feeling as if they were running in an ocean of honey, Roy made one last mental lunge for that paper number, 49, and his chute. He went spinning, tumbling, as if falling into a dark whirlpool that sucked him deeper and deeper into a peaceful, freeing numbness.

The recovery area was set up at the far end of the hotel lobby, the headquarters for the Bikila Memorial Marathon.

It was a vast towering interior, with a dramatically curved ceiling that looked down on giant columns of marble shooting up from a floor of more streaked marble. The rest of the field of four hundred was still trickling into the retreat of cool and quiet, their faces pale, their eyes sunken, fumbling with aid toward the cots, and it would be hours before the Bikila Memorial would throw up its last victim.

Roy listened to the hollow clicks of shoes and the hushed voices of guests out in the center of the lobby, all the little echoes, as he lay on a cot with his eyes closed. He could hear, too, the coughing, the moans, the scurrying of attendants from one limp body to the other, the splash of insides into buckets. There were no fans on the ceiling above them, only big-eyed, dark young boys all in white slapping two-handed breezes over the runners with fans shaped like stingrays.

Finally, he opened his bloodshot eyes. He had been carried in on a stretcher an hour before. Now a nurse flapped about him, dabbing once more at the skin burns and nicks suffered from his rolling fall into the chute. His mind ran over his whole flaring, skeletal frame; nothing unusual. He opened his eyes wider; he could see clearly. He twisted on his cot and looked down at the bucket of vomit; good color, not black like at . . . He chased the thought. He saw the tray of Perrier next to the nurse and pulled a bottle quickly to his mouth, letting the water dribble out over his lips and down his chest.

"Crazy, huh?" said Roy, after a long swig. The nurse said nothing. He wondered if the East German had seen him being carried in on the stretcher.

"How is he?" he asked, pointing across three cots at Overbeck. The nurse kept working on his cuts; she could only speak Amharic. Then he noticed the stretcher standing behind Overbeck's cot. He smiled and put his head back on the pillow.

His mind drifted, then came back with the suddenness of a fan being slapped across his face. He assayed his work in today's marathon, over this course—with its weather and terrain—that he had known long ago would bring him face to face with the fear that had buried itself so deep within him since Oslo. Through his sheer, primitive will to survive—and with the help of the East German, who had jolted him out of the ooze of self-pity, shocked him into seeing that it was always so easy to lose, to quit—he had run through his fear. But he knew it was still there, waiting, floating like a specter over the dream, the obsession of his life: the *two-hour* marathon.

Roy Holt and the great barrier of two hours were inseparable in the public mind. Coming back after Oslo—where he had knocked three minutes off the previous record of 2:08—he had drawn huge crowds everywhere in the States. They came out to see a man go too fast and crack in front of them like an egg. He had given them nothing but a man trying to work himself back into condition, yet because of the intensity of his dream, his vulnerability that was like a bullfighter's who must work too close to the horns, Roy was a bigger name than ever. But beyond the fans, among critics and other runners alike, there was the smug ridicule that accompanies a man who tries to resist the gravity of what is defined as possible.

Roy sat up and looked over once more at the big sign posting the times in the recovery area, reading from the top: Franz Overbeck, German Democratic Republic, 2 hrs,

10 mins, 30 secs; and then his own name, Roy Holt, U.S.A., 2 hrs, 10 mins, 34 secs. Roy made the leap from Ethiopia to Oslo in his head. Given the brutal conditions, he was sure now that he might have run better and faster today than at any time in his career. The thought of the two-hour barrier circled once more in his mind like a giant bird of prey. Very soon, he thought. Or never. He was twenty-nine years old. He was broke, more or less, whatever the hell that meant. At least he was broke by standards of his peers, people his age who had long been storming their way up the success ladder. All he could do—when he was all right—was run farther, faster than anybody in the world. He should care about the future. But he couldn't—not until he tried one more time to bring down the two-hour barrier and leave a mark on his craft.

He looked over at Franz Overbeck lying on his cot, flanked by the massive Kurt Mueller, his personal security man and close friend. Roy got up and made his way to Overbeck. He didn't know what he was going to say to him. They had only been mildly cordial back in Montreal. Yet he had the urge to make a connection, to see if there was any more to him than just a man who had spent all of his life since a little boy being pricked for blood samples, being wired up continually to the vast machinery of East German athletic science. He wanted to take his measure because, somehow, they would meet again and they might never have another chance to talk. As Roy sat down on the edge of the cot, they looked at each other warily.

There was silence, and then Roy said to his security man, "Don't look so nervous, Mueller. I'm not angry." Mueller grinned weakly.

Roy turned to Overbeck, who was still on his back. He

looked down at the bucket by the side of the cot. "You didn't even vomit, Franz," said Roy.

"He is fit," Mueller said.

"Four seconds," Roy said. "That's all."

Overbeck nodded, then looked up at Mueller, who shrugged and said, "Two fools."

"Kurt is not happy," Overbeck said in accented English.

"You could have hurt yourself today," Mueller said. "The weather. Your pace. Madness. Because of him." He nodded curtly at Roy.

"I didn't know you cared," Roy said.

"Four seconds," said the East German. "Enough. I played with you."

Roy said, smiling, "That water thing. Very cheap."

"We won," said Overbeck. "That is the result. You should know. You once would do anything to win."

"Nothing that cheap," Roy said, the smile gone. "But I'll tell you something. You beat me out there today, but you didn't win much. I won bigger."

"Congratulations," said Franz wryly.

"Will I see you in Boston?"

"What will be in Boston?"

"That's where I'm going to blow the marathon out of your reach," Roy said. Overbeck looked up at Mueller, as if looking for an answer to a riddle.

"Two hours," Mueller said. "What else? The American's pipe dream." They were speaking in German now, and then Franz took a long, patronizing look at Roy.

"You will never do it," Franz said. "Believe me."

"Why? It's hanging right out there, Franz. If you could speak for yourself, act for yourself, you'd go for it, too."

Franz shook his head. "Not by you."

"Who's run the marathon faster?" snapped Roy.

"I made you run today," Overbeck said. "You"—he weighed his words—"you do not know how to win anymore. I saw that today."

Roy stood up. "The German mind. So certain. So final." He began to walk away, then stopped. "I'll be there. I'd give anything to have you in Boston. You'd make a great spectator—running behind me."

They watched Roy move back to his cot. "Very desperate man, Roy Holt," said Mueller.

"Something happened to him in Oslo," Overbeck said. "I do not know what."

Roy was packing his things when he saw an Ethiopian official at the far end of the area, holding a piece of paper and shouting. He could not make out the words until the man drew closer. Then, hearing them clearly, he dropped down on his cot, stunned and staring blankly down the row of runners. The words throbbed in his head: *Attention! Attention! Kanji Sato, of Japan, has just set a new world's record for the marathon in Hiroshima—two hours, three minutes.* He threw the numerals up in his head: 2:03, two big, dramatic minutes off his own Oslo breakthrough. All heads in the recovery area turned toward Holt. Roy glared back at them.

What were they looking for? Anger? Defeat? Not here. You've done it for me, Kanji, thought Roy, as the afternoon shadows sliced through the high windows. Are you listening? They said it couldn't be done. What was the tag —Holt's Folly, the wildcat fantasy of a man with a damaged perspective since Oslo? Well, you've done it, Kanji, you've brought the two-hour marathon closer, put the hook in the fish. He wanted to get up and run forever. He bolted to his feet, then threw his left arm up in the air and launched into a glorious shriek that climbed one octave after another and bounced off the towering walls, startling the two leashed cheetahs that were standing on each side of the tall, uniformed Ethiopian on a podium facing the hotel's entrance. The cheetahs jumped at the sound: Kannnnnnnnnnnnnnnjiiiiiiiiiiiii!

The East Germans, bags in hands, froze on the other side and gaped at him.

"It must have been the sun," said Mueller.

Overbeck did not speak. He kept his ice-blue eyes on Holt, who was now sitting back and smiling. Why, he wondered, was he shouting about the Japanese? Why did Holt always seem to agitate him, thrust somehow through his heavily forged armor that remained untouched by emotion or passion? He looked at Holt as if he were a phenomenon. He was annoyed. He had put hurt on the American's body today; he had toyed with him like a cat with a ball of yarn. He wanted him to be suffering now; he wasn't. Holt's wail told him what he could never admit: his victory, indeed, had been small today. He started to walk toward the American.

"No," said Mueller, grabbing his arm.

"A moment," said Franz.

He moved toward Holt, then stood over him, saying, "You are no longer the fastest marathon man."

"Who is Sato?" asked Roy, not looking up.

Franz started to bend down, then changed his mind. "Listen to me, Roy," said Franz. He had never called him Roy before. "You do not like me. Nor I you."

"Kanji Sato," Roy interrupted. "Nobody will laugh now."

"Listen," Franz said. "We have made studies back at our

28

institute. It cannot be done. It is a death race. Two hours is a death race. Do you hear me?"

"Who is Kanji Sato?" Roy asked again, finally looking up.

"I could not care less," said the East German, turning abruptly away from the grinning American.

Their studies, thought Roy, watching the East German go. Plug in a computer, pile up the readouts, probe and prune and *pfff*, just like that: the marathon robot. One day, he knew, they'd have to define it in the record books, maybe use an asterisk to show who was robot and who was quaintly human. The East German couldn't care less, but he himself did. He had to care about a man named Kanji Sato who came out of nowhere—out of all the marathons being run around the world on this Sunday—to raise the level of the game.

2

Five days after the Hiroshima marathon, Kanji Sato stood at the window of the Buddhist monastery high above the long, winding road that trailed between the stormy Japan Sea and a range of snow-capped mountains. He felt a tap on his shoulder. The monk whispered, "It is time for you to go down." Kanji did not turn, but he said, "No, I will not be a part of it." The monk tried again. "Your father is dead. Have you no respect?" Kanji turned and burned his eyes into the monk. The monk went back to his mat, where he began praying.

Kanji raised his field glasses and let them move over the miles of villages that faced the wild shore, gray now in the early evening and so far from the "new Japan" that he despised, back there in Tokyo five hundred miles away. He envied his father for having been born in one of these villages, for having had such a place to remember so remote from the rich leather, the deep rugs and polished wood of his banking empire. He put down his glasses and listened: to the cresting wind, to the great chime in the shape of an ideograph under the heavenly arch, to the monk behind him chanting sutras for the dead.

Dark seemed instant, a signal for a long procession of Shinto priests and monks to move silently into sight below him, soon followed by his father's coffin being carried to the crematorium at the foot of the hills. Plainly outlined by blowing torch flame, the coffin was of pure white wood built in imitation of a temple, and it trailed a dragon's head with long streamers to scare away the devil. And still there was more: hired wailing mourners and white-robed priests carrying gleaming black paper lanterns. He turned away as the ceremony slipped under the arch. The chanting monk was once more next to him.

Looking at the dove, then into the face of the monk, Kanji said, "No." He knew it was his duty to take the dove, to put it in the cage standing by the window and then at the exact moment of cremation to send it soaring into the dark, carrying with it the symbol of his father's renewed life with his ancestors. The dove beat its wings, and the monk stroked it with his bony fingers. Once more, his eyes working deep into Kanji's, the monk offered the dove. Kanji looked down at the hands, then began to walk away, stopping only—without turning—to hear the monk's words.

"It is not right," said the monk.

"My father is not free," Kanji said. He then turned back to the monk and the dove. "I will free him. I will be back. It is not right for me to do it now."

"Now," said the monk, extending his hands again.

"One day," Kanji said.

"His ashes?" asked the monk.

"You keep them," Kanji replied. He walked quickly out of the room.

Down below in front of the monastery, Ichiro Gumbei stood next to a car and watched the last lantern fade down the hill. There was a tear in the corner of his eye, and now Kanji, standing next to him, noticed it but did not say anything. Kanji knew that face as well as his own; that was how he could notice the tear. No stranger could ever see emotion in that face, a rolling mass of hardened fat with two mailbox slits for eyes, which seemed to become even smaller when he was hungry. Quivering and heaving, his magnificent belly and the huge appendages on his chest indicated when he was laughing. If Ichiro was angry, his long neck, his downfall as a sumo wrestler, with its always-moist folds of accordion blubber burrowed deep into the cocoon formed by his wide shoulders—seemed to move out slowly like a turtle's head from his five hundred pounds. It took six yards of cloth to make him a shirt. It took three waiters to satisfy him in a restaurant. Kanji called him Ichy.

Kanji tossed him a handkerchief, and Ichy blew his nose. The sound brought a smile to Kanji's face. He looked up at the windows of the monastery. "That sounded like an earthquake here."

Ichy's chest shook, sending up the gasp of a man being strangled; he was laughing. Calmed, he said, "I can't help it. I loved that man."

"That's because he was not your father," said Kanji.

Ichy squeezed in behind the wheel of the big car, and Kanji got in beside him. Ichy sighed. "There is no need to hate him anymore."

"Hate?" said Kanji, shaking his head. "Why do you think I run?"

"Because you can," Ichy said, tapping his fat hand on the

wheel. He thought of his own three-year failure in the sumo ring. "Because you found something. Most never do."

"The marathon is a weapon," Kanji said. "Nothing more. Nothing less. I've told you that."

"But against what?"

"For the old one. For the grandson . . . my father." He began to say more, then stopped. "Drive," he said, closing his eyes. "To the inn-and-geisha house up the road."

Kanji's father, Yatero Sato, was the grandson of the legendary Takamori Sato, "the old one," the general who united the samurai from the Chosu and Satsuma fiefs and brought to an end in 1867 seven hundred years of feudal rule by the shoguns; he had returned the supreme power to the emperor. The old one had wanted progress, not potential subjugation by the West. Later, in 1877, he rebelled against the Meiji emperor's advisers, who were bringing Japan deep into Western ideas and customs. Gallant but outmanned, the old warrior was beaten and committed sep puku. He died with nobility and grace for what he believed to be the divine mission of his life and that of Japan's—to keep the emperor away from the treacherous West. He became—and remains—one of Japan's greatest heroes, and never more so than during World War II, when the code of the samurai fired the nation.

With the old one's rebellion smashed and the door flung open to the West, the samurai were in decline. But some of them, including the Satos, survived by shrewdly using their imaginations to gain footholds in business, hitherto a degrading pursuit. The Satos in Yatero's line became bankers. Yatero, born in 1903, was strictly raised in the godlike light of Takamori and the code of the samurai that insisted on

honor, dignity, purpose and rectitude in the face of dishon-
orable death. Out of university, Yatero joined the family's
banking empire, which was now reeling from the collapse
of the silk trade, largely due to the Depression in the
United States, a large customer.

Came 1931, Yatero was the first in the family to see the
benefit of aligning with the militarism of the jingoes and
the growing nationalism among politicians. Quietly, he
went about building a bridge between the *zaibatsu*—the
old-line financial and industrial cartel—and the generals
who were ready to pounce on Manchuria. Quickly, the
Sato banks acquired certain franchises in the new puppet
state of Northern China after the invasion, helping the business to rally dramatically; Yatero's prestige was high.

By 1940, after war erupted in Europe, distracting the col-
onial powers from Asia, Yatero became the leader in the
formation of the Greater East Asia Co-Prosperity Sphere,
another divine mission of Japan. When General Hideki
Tojo became prime minister in 1941, he named Yatero to
direct economic cohesion within the Sphere, which was
rapidly coming under imperial rule. Yatero was now the
hand on the Japanese war machine. He stood on the balco-
nies of one captured city after another, secure in his vision:
a Japanese Asia and all the riches that came with it.

Yatero's brokership came down around him five years
later amid horrible testimony: radiation death and a humili-
ated people whose ruling principle had always been to
avoid humiliation. Postwar Japan saw General Douglas
MacArthur drain off the emperor's deified glow and then
strip the *zaibatsu* of its power and thrust in affairs. Yatero
was over forty now, and he waited for his death sentence.
It never came; nobody knew why. Perhaps it was due to the

lack of his visibility. He spent a year in jail, then was loosed in a culture in which ten thousand people all over Japan had killed themselves when the Americans entered Tokyo. The people wanted to see him dead; honor demanded it.

Freed from prison, Yatero was begged by his wife to commit suicide with her. She poured poison for herself and passed him the blade. He would not comply. Weeping and screaming, she ran into the streets, calling him a coward, and soon killed herself by jumping in front of a train. She left a note that pointed to her shame for him as the reason. The story was played up in the papers. Yatero's house was burned down. He was spat on in public. But as the years went by and the Occupation hardships lessened, the *zaibatsu* and Yatero Sato were recycled to the forefront of the reviving Japanese economy. He married again and fathered Kanji in 1953. He had vowed that his son would be a man of the West.

The inn-geisha house was a horseshoe of rectangular buildings joined by long corridors, embracing a large rock garden that had red and yellow flowers, a waterfall and cherry trees that tinkled with wind-bells made of tiny pieces of broken glass. Inside, Kanji and Ichy sat silently on the high bench in the sauna; it was not the quiet of mourning, just that of two men without anything to say for the moment. The upper halves of their bodies were wreathed with steam, and now a woman attendant brought in a bucket of water and poured it on the hot stones slowly, her eyes crinkling with a smile as they moved down from Ichy's abdomen, a mountain that jutted out and would have hid his testes had they not hung like those of an elephant.

35

"The American is back," said Kanji, his face hidden by the steam.

"What American?" Ichy asked.

"Roy Holt," said Kanji. "He was once the best. It was his record I broke at Hiroshima."

"Where has he been?" Ichy grunted.

"What does he want?" Kanji wondered aloud. He knew the answer before the question was out. "Two hours. That's it! He'll try to go for it. Where? When?"

Ichy shifted his body, the cloud of steam dispersing around him.

"Boston. That's it!" Kanji jumped down from his perch. "Five months from now. He wouldn't just come back for a race. Not him. He wants it all now. The barrier. Or nothing."

Kanji tried to light the image of the American in his head; it had been so long ago. Now he had it: six feet and, say, two inches; powerful, short torso on long, thin legs; curly auburn hair; a sharp-boned face with a pair of amused eyes that always seemed to say he was glad to be doing the only thing he ever wanted to do in life. But beneath his easy presence, his carefree nature, Holt was ruthless with himself and others, fearless of time or distance. He did not merely run a marathon; he destroyed it, crushed it, then watched it dribble out of his fist. There was a luminous quality to Roy Holt, a sureness of purpose, something of the warrior about him.

"Formidable," said Kanji, doing push-ups. "That's Holt. I saw him in Montreal against the East German. They said he didn't have a chance against Franz Overbeck. Holt left him in shreds."

Ichy grunted again. Kanji stood up, then breathed deeply and felt the heat in his lungs. He berated himself for thinking so highly of the American. He had never liked Americans since his first studies in Japanese history. He had liked them even less after his father sent him to Yale. He left after two years, having seen nothing to change his mind that the Americans—since the days of Commodore Perry —had viewed his own people cheaply, had thought of them as little, *yellow*—not white—people with bowed legs who lived in a miniature world of childish rites. The American Immigration Act of 1924 alone was a bitter example of prejudice aimed directly at his people. Even MacArthur had betrayed the American attitude when he said: "The Japanese are like twelve-year-olds."

He fixed his mind on Holt again. Having created the picture of him, Kanji now threw himself into the frame. He was standing next to the American now. He didn't like what he saw: a hard body, all right, but sawed off to five feet, six inches, held up by a pair of slightly bowed legs; he cursed that genetic slight in the Japanese. He went on: short, cropped hair, sharp eyes, a face that seemed to be out of a mold and could never be disassembled by any emotion, almost the same visage as the old one, his grandfather Takamori Sato, whom he loved so much. He was no match, he thought, for the American in looks, but . . .

"He'll be there!" blurted Kanji. "I know it!"

Kanji began pacing the sauna. Ichy squinted down at him. He was glad to see him excited. There had been a curious deadness about him since his race in Hiroshima. Ichy didn't know much about the marathon. He knew only about Kanji, how to be his friend, how to protect him, ever since they were young boys. That was what Yatero had wanted from Ichy. When Ichy wanted to become a sumo wrestler, the father threw his financial support behind him, never once mocking his dismal career and saying only a few words when Ichy quit: "Kanji is your work now. You are not a retainer. You are a brother to him."

Finished in the sauna, they took a cold shower, and attendants led them to a pair of brass tubs in another room. They sat there, not talking, and soaked for a while, and then they stood up as the girls soaped them heavily, their hands squishing in and out of the secret passages of their customers' bodies, each girl and man impervious to the sexuality of it. It was a rite that was as simple and as basic as bread being put on a table, and one that seldom failed to flush the cheeks of Western men and women. Distracted from his thoughts briefly, Kanji looked over at Ichy and smiled as both girls combed the soap off the giant sumo wrestler. He looked like a melting snowman.

Dressed in kimonos, they were led to the geisha rooms inside the inn. They were greeted at the sliding doors by two geishas, who sat them down on a tatami mat on each side of a low table. Across from Kanji, Ichy stared at the large container of sake. The geisha next to Ichy began to pour. Kanji watched him bolt down ten cups rapidly, listening to his easygoing chatter with the geisha. His own geisha seemed more in the classic mold, self-effacing, demure, refined in oblique conversation, cleverly charming, not a whore, as most Westerners thought, but a courtesan who planned carefully for her future. Kanji grabbed the sake. He drank heavily. He wanted to be in the party.

"You never drink," said Ichy warily.

"I do now," said Kanji, wiping his mouth.

He drank more at dinner, becoming louder and stubbornly egotistical, two things he never was. "I'll tell you . . . right now, Ichy," he slurred. "If Holt shows up in Boston, I'll cut him in two." He raised both hands together as if he were holding the katana, the long, exquisite blade that was the magical symbol of the samurai. He struggled to his feet and made a wide sweep with the imaginary blade. "Hip to hip!" yelled Kanji. "Just like Takamori, my grandfather. Hip to hip!" The geishas just laughed; they did not understand English. Ichy told him to sit down. But Kanji made the wide sweep once more and then fell down.

Ichy's whole body was jiggling, the fat heaving on his chest, as he picked Kanji up. Kanji was not laughing. The geishas were silent. Ichy's body went still.

"His whole career," said Kanji, "was a total of seconds." Kanji moved closer to Ichy, circling his too long neck with his arms. The sweat poured over the folds of Ichy's face. The geishas listened to the two men grunt. Then Kanji backed off.

"But, aaah, the belly!" said Kanji. "That is of more interest. Do you know what they say about Ichy's belly? No man can budge him with a kick to the belly." He looked down at Ichy's belly. "Perfection. Greatness. But, sadly, they do not kick in sumo."

Ichy shook his head, then used his chopsticks to bring a single grain of rice from his bowl into the maw of his mouth. The eyes of the geishas fastened on him.

"And you would see no pain on his face, either," said Kanji. "In the training halls of sumo, they say he is a marvel. Shall we see for ourselves, ladies?"

Ichy tilted his head up to Kanji. "No," said Ichy.

"Then it is not true what they say," said Kanji. "You have only a fat man's belly. A useless, bottomless pit."

"It is true," said Ichy. "I have the greatest belly in all of Japan." The sake was finally beginning to reach him.

"Get up," said Kanji. "Show us."

"No," said Ichy. "You are drunk."

"Get up, you mountain of grease! Get over there!" The order, the sting of the words, made Ichy's head twitch. He was growing angry. He could still hear Kanji shouting. It took him a while, but he untwined his crossed legs and lumbered over to the other side of the room. He took off his kimono, then his shirt. The eyes of the geishas grew wide as they saw the mass of suet spill out. He then squatted, his hands on his knees, and looked at Kanji.

"Come on, you bastard," grumbled Ichy.

Kanji was struck by the sudden anger, then approached him. He was ready to forget it all, but on impulse brought his leg back and sent it hard into Ichy's belly. He looked for a reaction; there was none. He lined up the belly again and rammed his pointed foot dead center into where Ichy's navel might be. The giant didn't even sway. Again and again he dug his foot into the gullied fat, and then Ichy was laughing, his shoulders shaking, his breasts flopping. Kanji rubbed his knee, feeling a searing twinge. Enraged at the laughing, he started to kick again, then suddenly stopped. He walked back and picked up the geisha's samisen, a guitarlike Japanese instrument. He smashed it three times over Ichy's head before it shattered, leaving splinters and guitar strings and cuts on the giant's head. Ichy had not flinched.

Kanji fell down on his knees before Ichy, who was sobbing now. He stayed there for a moment, then finally rose.

"Forgive me," said Kanji.

"It was the drink," said Ichy, standing up. The geishas rushed up and began cleaning the cuts on his forehead.

"No," said Kanji. "I know better."

He embraced Ichy and walked out into the garden of the inn, almost sober now. He sat there listening to the windbells, staring at the rocks and feeling the cool wind drying the sweat on his face. The *haji*, the great shame he felt for his father, was even stronger now after his death.

By his failure to commit seppuku after the war, his father, a blooded samurai, had accepted the grace of the enemy, an unpardonable breach of conduct for a samurai, for a man who had led his nation into war. The judgment of the people was clear. He was a sullied man, impure and unworthy of their respect. Despite his grandfather Takamori's mythic stature, Kanji was made keenly aware of his father's role in history from his earliest days in school. While young, Kanji had tried to make excuses to himself for his father's actions, but he had soon replaced his presence with the memory of Takamori. For all his mother's efforts to bring them closer together before her death, the curtain of shame had remained between Kanji and his father.

Hoping to free himself from the shame, Kanji went on to become an ardent nationalist. By running, he brought focus to his ideas and his lineage, citing his grandfather as the spiritual force within him. Like all other people, the Japanese love a good yarn, especially one with a touching, tragic element in it: *shinju*, the double suicide of two lovers who are kept apart by their families; the suicide of a student over failure in exams; the man shunned by society; the person who kills himself out of honor or social concern. And now here was the story of Kanji Sato, a man caught between the glory of Takamori and the shade of his father; the press dredged it up each time Kanji ran in a marathon.

"You are using me," Yatero had said six months before, the last time that they would talk.

"I am trying to bring honor to your name," said Kanji.

"I am dying," said his father. "I will be free soon."

"Yes," said Kanji, "but I will be here."

Yatero waved him out of the room. "Honor to you is

41

only words. What do you know about life and death? Is there life and death in this . . . this . . . marathon?"

"It is my sword," said Kanji.

Now, sitting in the garden alone, Kanji could hear his father's words, see himself rejecting the dove in the monk's palms, his last act of ingratitude, of disrespect toward his father, could feel the frustration of the moment that had turned in to the rage hurled at Ichy.

Kanji's eyes moved from the garden. Ichy came out and sat down. "The knee. Let me see it."

"Just aches a little," said Kanji.

"I'll get some ice," said Ichy.

"No, it was just a twist. It will be fine in the morning. Your cuts?"

Ichy shrugged.

"I am sorry," said Kanji.

"Nothing."

Kanji stood up, then looked down at Ichy. "Could you cut off my head?" He studied his reaction. "Could you . . . for me?"

There was silence, and Ichy said, "Now? Or can we wait until tomorrow?"

Their laughter filled the dark garden, and then Ichy helped Kanji limp to his room.

3

The East Germans had laid over in Prague for a few days, and now the train was moving across the Czech border and into East Germany toward Leipzig, home of the Lenin Sports Institute. Lying in flat country, Leipzig was known as the home of Bach and the poet Schiller and as far back as medieval times was one of the bustling trade centers of the world. Now the city was renowned for its export of Siberian tigers and furs—and the athletes shaped by the Institute, a vital and expensive priority of the German Democratic Republic.

The Institute was a powerhouse of brains and efficiency. It had fifty doctors, a hundred technicians, an eighty-man security unit and any number of trainers and instructors to oversee the work of its three hundred athletes. But beyond the head count, nobody in the West really knew what went on inside the complex, except that it was surely another all-out effort of the Teutonic mind to conquer the tricky seas of human life and personality, to produce athletes like Franz Overbeck.

Franz sat in his compartment, looking out as the train glided past the plain now dotted with monuments, where Field Marshal Blücher's forces had turned back Napoleon in 1813. He was glad to be going home, back to the Institute, then up to the sports camp in the Harz Mountains, where he had lived and trained for most of his twenty-eight years, where the routine battered down the memories of his wife, Greta, where his reputation and sense of self-value helped fight the pain of her loss. Gone now for two years—a defector to America—she had nearly ruined his life, and it had taken months to ease an emotion that had been new to him and would have been startling to those who thought they knew him.

Kurt Mueller opened the door, sat down and began chewing absently on a hunk of sausage. Sharply muscled, with an angular face and sandy hair, aged forty, Mueller was a crack and trusted security man, one of the few field men who answered only to Emile Zweig, the head of the security force. Mueller lived well in Leipzig, with a wife and three children. He had been the top man at several Olympics but was assigned solely to Franz Overbeck since Greta's defection. He alone knew of Franz's silent hurt over Greta. He was more than a watchdog. He was a sympathetic friend.

"Thinking again?" Mueller asked, speaking in German.

"Of the Japanese," Franz lied. "Is he real?"

"Tiny course," Mueller mocked, waving his hand. "Tiny people. Nonsense. Like Roy Holt's two hours."

"Holt is finished," said Franz.

"You should be thinking about Otto Albrecht," Mueller said. "He's going to want some answers about Ethiopia."

"Otto talks. I listen."

"Otto knows everything. You'd think he would rely on

our security. No, not him. He's got spies all over the place up at the camp."

"I don't know any spies."

"You're not supposed to. That is the idea. Take your friend Willy. Watch it. You never know."

"Willy Schmidt is harmless. If I didn't watch out for him, who would?"

"Just the same. . ."

"Who, Kurt?" Franz broke in, now sitting on the edge of the seat. The question was clear to Mueller. He'd been hearing it for months now. He had known it was coming as soon as he entered the compartment, could see it in Franz's empty eyes. He'd seen the look often lately.

"You have to stop asking," said Mueller.

"Who helped Greta get out?" pressed Franz.

"What's the point? She got out. It could have happened a hundred ways." Mueller looked away. "Forget her." The words were hollow to him. A man could never forget a woman like Greta, not even the impenetrable Franz Overbeck, the recognized model of Institute behavior. Mueller knew he was bound to report what he saw or thought. Yet he never could. He trusted Franz; Greta would pass. It would just take a little time. Franz would be his old self again, selfish and fired with allegiance to the program.

Franz's uncle Heinrich was there to meet him at the Leipzig station. Kurt was going to spend a couple of days with his family, so Heinrich had come down from the sports camp in the Harz Mountains to drive him back up to the compound. Franz lived up there with his uncle, the only family he had left, in the best cabin on the grounds; it had once been home for Greta and Franz.

Heinrich was a short, corpulent man, given to heavy food and drink. He had spent his first forty years in Munich, then come to Leipzig to raise Franz following his father's death and his mother's sudden desertion. Heinrich had lived recklessly in Bavaria, dealing first in the black market and then as a "minor ear" for the West at the Cafe Europa—a meeting place for second-rate agents.

Before joining Franz, the uncle had done a few "turns" for the East Germans, and when he made the leap from Munich to Leipzig—from gaiety to austerity—he had had no trouble. He also took with him all the names of the third-string agents in Bavaria—given to him, of course, by their own controls. Heinrich could be valuable to the West as a resident in East Germany.

Heinrich was well over sixty now and looked upon as a harmless old fool. He was always listening to country music and the tapes of Donna Summer, usually smuggled back by Franz after a trip abroad. As long as he was discreet, the Sports Federation had no interest in his taste in music or his treasure of *Playboy* centerfolds, which lined the walls of his cabin room; senility was unpredictable.

Besides, the Federation thought that Heinrich was good for Franz: a boost to his ego, a comic distraction from the void left by Greta. There were only two strict requests. He was to be seen in no pictures with Franz, and he was never to wear a track suit; the Federation viewed his ungainly figure as a contradiction to the growing fear elsewhere of East German physical superiority. Heinrich didn't care. He wasn't an East German. He was a German, a Bavarian, and if the East Germans wanted to mistake that for senility it was all right with him. He liked being underestimated.

Now, behind the wheel of the car, Heinrich turned on

the tape recorder on the seat between him and Franz and listened to the sensual voice of Donna Summer.

"Listen to her," Heinrich said, drumming his fingers on the wheel. "A goddess." He looked at Franz out of the corner of his eye. "What a body! Just think about it. To be young and in America. Sex in the air. Excitement. Discos at night. Asses wiggling." He clasped his hands prayerfully, raised his eyes to the car roof. "Just once!"

"Keep your hands on the wheel," Franz said.

The car moved out of the city and into the countryside, and Heinrich said, "You crushed the American like a paper cup."

"Not exactly," Franz said. "But whatever he had left, I took it from him in Ethiopia. He doesn't have much more to give."

"He was never in your class," Heinrich said, jiggling his head with the music.

Franz thought for a few moments, then said, "Who got Greta out?"

Heinrich said, "You keep asking. But I don't have the answer to that question, Franz."

"You know who made the connection."

"And if I did," Heinrich said, "what good would it do? You'd turn him in, is that it? Or are you planning to take a trip yourself?"

"And if I was?"

"Then . . ." Heinrich stopped, and said, "Not you, Franz. You're a believer."

"And what do you believe in?"

"You," Heinrich said.

"I miss her badly," Franz said.

"I know."

47

"Would you help . . . if I wanted to take a trip?"

"If," Henrich said, looking over at him. "There are no ifs in a trip like that. You do it or you don't."

"Does Kurt know who helped her?"

"Kurt doesn't know."

"But you do. You were close to Greta."

The Donna Summer tape ended, and Heinrich said, putting on a new cartridge, his hand fumbling nervously, "How about a little Dolly Parton? Beautiful!

Franz put his head back on the seat and closed his eyes.

If Otto Albrecht had a favorite—and it was doubtful—that athlete was Franz Overbeck. As head of track and field, Albrecht had helped make East German athletics a powerful propaganda commodity. He kept a sharp eye on the rest of his three hundred athletes, but he looked upon Overbeck as the focus for his own driving ambition, for obvious reasons: the marathon was the most popular track event in the world right now, and Franz Overbeck was its monarch. He was the show window to the world for the East German way of doing things.

"America has its wheat," Albrecht had once said in a moment of rare spirit, "the Russians their cursed vodka, the Arabs their oil . . . and we have our own trademark—our athletes, our muscle and will."

Otto did not care for the Russians. There was no balance to their minds; they were given to dramatic swings of mood. He had always thought that if East Germany had to be a Communist state, then it ought to be German communism.

It all seemed so fitting to him, so typical of the German race, this creating of bone and muscle to live up to an ideal that went as far back as Barbarossa and Siegfried. To this end—as well as his own—he worked long hours, watching, measuring, feeling for cracks in the edifice, searching for the stray. The individual, the soaring ego, were his enemy. The malingerer could drive him to rage. The man who failed mocked the program—and Otto Albrecht.

Faced with a problem athlete, Albrecht's retaliation was always the same: the job and apartment taken away from the parents, the cutting off of the athlete from the identity that he had worked years to build. Few ever had to feel his whip.

"Who has no enemies!" one chorus of long-distance runners would sing out in training.

"Otto has no enemies!" the other chorus would answer, their laughter filling the spare woods of the Harz Mountains.

Surely, after eight years as the whip of track and field, Otto Albrecht's day was coming. He heard the knock on the door.

"Come in!" He didn't look up. "Good afternoon, Herr Overbeck." He traced his finger down a chart before him. Finished, he looked up at Overbeck, studying him as if he were a stranger.

"Sit," said Albrecht. "And tell me about your trip."

"No problems, sir. I never make trouble."

"Of course not. Not like some. They go out of the country. They complain about the security. They break the rules. They never go again. Even the best are expendable." He paused. "There is so much talent." He knew that was not true for the marathon. "Marathoners are made, not born, you know. Much work and money has gone into the making of Franz Overbeck."

"I agree, sir."

"Then you will also agree that it was a very foolish thing you did in Africa. You and the American."

"It was a hard race."

"No, Herr Overbeck." He wagged his forefinger as if correcting a child. "My trainers tell me. You made it personal. You played with Roy Holt. How else could a broken man come so close?"

"He was the best once," said Franz. He listened to his small defense of the American; it sounded odd to him.

"A sick man since Oslo. He ruined himself with his mania for speed, for two hours."

"He's going to try again," said Franz, thinking back to Holt's face when he had heard the news from Japan.

Albrecht jabbed his thumb down hard on his desk. "The American . . . the American! Holt is of no matter to you! Why has he always bothered you?"

"I don't know, sir."

"I know. Montreal! You've never been able to get that race out of your head."

"You're right."

"What is the sense? An old hand like you. *Once. Was.* That is the American now."

"I understand, sir."

"But do you? You have never been a man of personal feelings. There is no such word as 'personal.' I have never had to tell you that. You have been with us since you were a young boy. The program, Herr Overbeck. That is all that counts. You are vital to it." He quickly switched the topic. "Have you heard from her lately?" He could not bear to say the name.

"I never read Greta's letters," Franz said, telling what was the truth up until three months ago. "I tear them up."

"Very wise. Where is she living?" Franz knew Albrecht

had that answer. He knew every line in the letters, her desperate loneliness over their separation, her hope and love. The path of the letters was obvious, from security to Albrecht to himself.

"New York," Franz said.

"She betrayed us all," Albrecht said, adding, "You can leave now, Herr Overbeck. Mind our little talk today."

As Franz closed the door, Albrecht tapped his sunken cheek with his finger. Overbeck did not care for the bitch anymore. He was certain of that because of the reports from his spy in the camp. But that stubborn, capricious woman . . . he would always have to keep her firmly in his mind. If she ever came to Europe, he would retrieve her briskly. Like a dirk pulled out of a cuff, a thin, sharp smile crossed his face at the prospect. He knew her exact address, her every move, that lovely, golden sprinter who had nearly destroyed his career and had kept him in front of a board of inquiry for days. She should be killed right now, he thought, if only as an example to others. She made him anxious, like a man who had been robbed once and was always wondering if he had locked the door at night, even when he was certain he had.

Greta Overbeck leaned against the window of her New York apartment, watching the midnight rain dance in the streetlights on Twenty-seventh Street off Third Avenue. There was a temporary air to her three-and-a-half rooms, as if she was about to leave any moment. Her luggage stood in a corner, and her passport was handy on her writing table. The rooms were neat and clean, a little stark for a young woman with her looks, but an honest reflection of her salary and work as a gym instructor at a private girls' school on the upper East Side; it was only a stopgap job while she waited for a post with the U.S. Information Agency in Washington, where she would do broadcasts to Iron Curtain countries.

She closed the window curtain and walked to the closet mirror, wearing only a towel around her neck, her body still moist from the shower. As always, she let her eyes do the first search, and then her hands followed, moving carefully over her breasts, belly and thighs. Then she passed a finger evenly over her upper lip. For the last two years, every evening before going to bed, she had gone through these motions; it was not so much out of anxiety anymore as it was a habitual way of reminding herself that her decision to leave Franz had been right and honest. She saw nothing new—or old. There were no more tiny circles of black hair on her pale body or shadowy down over her full lip. But had it been worth all this emptiness? She was not sure anymore. She fluffed her damp hair with the towel and wondered what her husband would think of its length; he had only known her with short hair.

It had been two years since Greta had left Franz and East Germany, not long after her second miscarriage. They had been married in 1975 and gone on to the Montreal Olympics in 1976. From their first day in Montreal, attention poured over Greta, who was a stunning denial that all East German women athletes had hatchet faces and longshoremen's bodies. The networks' roving cameras had stayed with her even long after she won the gold medal in the hundred-meter sprint. Her beauty, her face, were the story.

If the East Germans were now in the beauty business, so were the journalists, even the old cranks. Their enthusiasm for Greta flowed. She did not just have a pretty woman's face. It came from a sculptor, the bones positioned by one who had the touch of a watchmaker and the eye of an eagle. Her bright green eyes were the work of a master diamond cutter. But most of all it was her skin of fine ivory, the feel of which was there without touching. Her gold medal always seemed parenthetical.

Greta was twenty-one back then. Five years later, life as a gold-medal sprinter at the Institute had drained her: the hundreds of needles that had been poked into her skin; the biomechanic testing, one doctor after another combing through her body and mind; the deadly routine. And most of all the dread steroids—given to increase strength before each big competition. She blamed the loss of her babies on the steroids. Home from Moscow, where she had won another gold medal, she noticed a patch of dark hair on her thigh no bigger than a quarter. She had run naked into the living room of their small cabin in the Harz Mountains.

"Franz! Franz!" There was terror in her eyes. "Look! My God, look!" She began to cry.

"Now, be calm," said Franz, holding her in his arms. He then looked down at her thigh. "It's nothing. It will go away soon."

"They're doing something to me!" she sobbed. "I am changing. I'll never be able to have any children."

He wiped away her tears with his sleeve. "You're still beautiful." He didn't know what else to say.

"I don't care about my beauty," she said, pushing him away and knowing then she had made her decision. Her life as an East German athlete was costing too much. She could not spend her life as an experiment. Somehow, she thought, she must get Franz to act with her.

She tried later to find a soft spot in his attitude. "Do you ever think about the West?" she asked while walking through the woods one night.

"You mean America?" Franz said.

"Yes. Do you ever wonder how they live there?"

"The cities are dirty. The people kill each other. No discipline. I couldn't live there."

"Would you just like to see it?"

Franz smiled. "Sure, Albrecht will send us tomorrow. He hates America."

"I would go right now," Greta said.

"Stop joking."

"I'm not. You mean you would not leave with me?" Franz stopped walking, and Greta began to laugh nervously.

"Never," Franz said. "I mean it. I don't like talk like this."

After that night, Greta was cautious. She could never put Franz in the middle by telling him of her plans. If she knew her husband at all, she was certain of several things: his love for her, his devotion to the Institute and his pride in his reputation. He neither knew or wanted any other life. Given a choice between that life and her, he would not give her away, but, she wondered, would he go with her? She could only wait for the final moment, then rely on his love for her. But she must not weaken in those few minutes that would be left to them.

The chance came during a trip to Paris to receive an award; as husband and wife, they were viewed as good security risks, and surveillance was limited. She only had two days. She had a phone number. The voice on the other end of the line gave her the time and the place, then the phone clicked. The next day she walked into the bedroom of their hotel suite, her eyes on the clock next to their bed. Franz, lying on the bed, was addressing postcards.

"Darling, I am going," Greta said.

"Where?" Franz asked, not looking up.

She drew in her breath and said, "To America. Come with me."

He kept writing. "Greta, I told you. No jokes."

"I'm not."

Franz looked up. He saw her standing by the door. She had no luggage.

"Please be serious, Greta," he said.

"I am, Franz. I am leaving. Just get up and come with me. I need you, darling."

"Come back here and sit down!" he shouted.

She moved backward to the door. "You must come with me!" The tears dropped down her cheeks.

He began to reach for the phone. "I'll call security."

"No, you won't. You're not that kind of man."

He pulled his hand from the phone and got up from the bed in one leap. "What would you do there alone? In that place."

She held her arms out to him. "Now, Franz."

"Why are you doing this? Because of a little hair? A few needles? Vanity. That's not you."

"My nerves, Franz. I can't live like that. I'm not made like you. I want another life." She kept her eyes on the clock. "God knows what they've done to my body." Her lips quivered.

"No clothes," he said. "No money. Just relax." He moved toward her. She opened the door.

"Stop me, and I'll never forgive you."

"I can't go," Franz said. "I can't dismiss my life. I just can't."

"And I . . ."

"Give me your hand, Greta." He reached for her.

"I'm going!"

"Greta!"

He watched her run to the elevator. He wanted to scream after her but quickly caught himself. After all, he thought, she would return in a few hours. It was only the strain of training, the depression still there from losing the babies. Greta was a strong woman; she would gain control of herself. She would never dare leave without him. He went back to his postcards, worried but confident. He'd give her a couple of hours, and if she wasn't back he'd send the security people after her.

Downstairs in front of the hotel, a limousine pulled up, and she saw the arm wave to her. She walked calmly over and stepped into the back seat. Her eyes were red and puffy now. She sat there quietly while the car moved through Paris. Finally, the man next to her said, "Are you all right?"

"He wouldn't come," she said.

"I'm sorry," said the man.

They rode for a while, and then the man said, "We're going to Marseilles. And from there to New York. You'll be all right. We'll look after you."

"What do I have to do for you?" asked Greta.

"You've already done it," said the man. "You've left them. For us."

Now, two years later, she climbed into her bed and pulled the covers up to her neck. After the first few weeks of steady publicity, the television shows and press conferences, she was allowed to settle down. She almost missed the attention now. She was always alone. She saw no one, except for the two funny men she called the Smith Brothers who were from the government and had been so kind to her. They were still in touch with her socially—or was it their job?—and often she could sense that they were following her, not as much as in her early days but still there.

She turned off the light and listened to the autumn storm outside, certain now that she and Franz should have another chance at life, even if she had to go back to East Germany. He would have to reject her once more. Their separation in Paris had been too quick, too charged with her emotion. She began to berate herself. She had been selfish. She had hurt him badly. She would have to act soon. Her skin was hot. She moved her hand up her thigh, and for a moment he was lying next to her. Then, minutes later, she gasped, and he was gone.

4

They stood there looking through the fence of the Central Park reservoir, watching the first light of morning drop down on the water. The heavyweight wore a pair of army boots and a gray rubber jacket with the hood up, and sweat dripped off his black mustache onto the sleeve of Roy's scuffed pilot jacket. Roy liked fighters; they were good for him, they made him feel quick and hard inside. He liked running with them in the morning, liked the smell and feel- of the gym down on Fourteenth Street, where he had spent a lot of afternoons over the last year and a half.

"How many more?" asked the heavyweight, putting a finger to each side of his nose and snorting.

"Couple more," said Roy.

"Why, Roy, we did four miles!" The fighter stamped his big foot playfully.

"Danny says six," Roy said. "I gotta see six. You know he'll ask me."

The fighter shook his head. "Nigger like me . . . I don't know what I'm doin' out here with the cocks crowin'."

"Don't call yourself that," Roy said.

"Anybody but you, Roy, I'd say bullshit. White man don't have a right to tell a black man he can't call himself a nigger."

"Suit yourself," Roy said. "I'm not a social worker."

"I know you mean it, Roy."

"What's it feel like?" Roy asked, his mind going back to Oslo. "When you get tagged? You've been there, right?"

"Been there!" He laughed. "I owwnnn the place. I ain't never lost a fight on a decision. And I done lost seven of my last ten."

"You ever get gun shy? You know . . . like, Christ, I don't want any more of that pain."

"It's just a little old black spot. A fighter, he don't like to talk about it much. But me . . . hell, I ain't gone nowhere but back down on my ass. You've been there?"

"Yeah, I've been there," Roy said.

The heavyweight belonged to Honest Dan Neeley. So did the gym and the five-story apartment house, a frayed little walk-up on the West Side; Roy lived on the top floor. He'd met Dan when he first came to New York. The old guy was trying to leg his bike up a big hill in the park. Jogging behind him, Roy had seen the bike begin to sway and the man lose control. He had turned it around and was biking downhill when the front wheel jackknifed, sending the man and his head to the ground right near Roy. He rushed over to the man. His nose was scraped, and there was a cut above his eye dripping blood on his hand. He sat there dazed, and Roy offered to call an ambulance. The man refused, got up and kicked the bike. Shakily, the man asked Roy to help him home.

"Honest Dan Neeley's the name," he said. "Forget the Honest. I'd steal a boxcar if I could carry it." He kicked the bike again.

Dim and cluttered, the room was on the fourth floor in the back of the house. The place was filled with sparring headgear, swab sticks, a few water pails, a couple of dusty satchels and rolls of tapes. Dan reached into one of the satchels, pulled out a bottle of solution, gave Roy a swab stick out of a box and told him to clean the cut over his eye. Finished, he watched the old guy handle the wound. He was a little blade of a man, with a pair of quick, hooded eyes. There was a choppy clip to his words, which came out of the side of his mouth.

"Butterflies," Danny said, inserting clamps over his cut, drawing the flesh together. "Good as stitches." Roy's eyes moved toward a pair of blood-stained trunks under a large picture of a fighter on the wall.

"Rocky Marciano," Danny said. "Ever hear of him? Walcott versus Marciano." He made a face. "Nasty night. The Rock had his nose split. Blood all over the place. I was in the corner. Assistant trainer then. That nose! Made you wanna cry. He gutted it out. Don't make 'em like the Rock anymore, do they?"

"You all right?" asked Roy. Danny nodded. Then I'll be going now," said Roy.

"Hold on," said Danny. He looked at the sticky blood on his fingers. "Hah, that's what I get. Stop smoking, read the obituaries too much, and you wanna be Superman." Roy got up to leave. Danny said, "Say, kid, what can I do for ya, huh?"

"Nothing," Roy said. "Glad to help."

"You kiddin'? In this town! If you didn't pick me up, I'd still be lyin' there. With my pockets turned out. What's your game, kid?"

"I'm a runner."

"You run numbers?"

"I run in marathons."

"Marathons . . . you dance in 'em?"

Roy smiled. "Long-distance running. I'm from Ohio."

"Nobody's from Ohio. College?"

"Yeah. Out six years. Never had time to build a career. It's been the marathon. That's all. I just got in town a few days ago. I'm staying at the Y."

"You stayin' around a while?"

"Yeah. I'm going to try and hook onto some night job. Like a watchman."

"You got it, kid," said Danny, grinning. "Stop lookin'. Between the gym downtown, this house and my fighters, I do all right."

"You a fight manager?"

"Yeah. Not like I once was. But I'm in action. Couple of heavies treat me fine. Got a middle who'll be ready for TV soon. About six more who try hard but . . . well, they gotta make a livin', too."

"What's the work?" Roy asked.

"Light work around the house here. Run some in the morning with my fighters. Not every day. They'll cheat if I let 'em, you know. And work in the gym with me. You know, getting the fighters ready. For their sparring. Rubbin' their faces with Vaseline. I'll teach you."

Roy thought for a moment. "You know I have to train myself. Then I'll be traveling sometimes."

"No problem," said Danny. "Here's what you get. The

three rooms up from me. Fifth floor back. Rent free. And a hundred bucks a week. Deal?"

Roy extended his hand. "You're on, Danny."

Upstairs after the run, Roy picked at his food, cleaned the dishes and then sat down in the living room. He couldn't help thinking of Amy. She had been slight, intense, always driving toward the future. She and Buck Lewis, his college coach, had been a double anchor in his life. He remembered a few words long ago between Buck and Amy, not long after he had won the gold medal in Montreal.

"Buck?" she asked. "Can Roy be a top marathoner?"

"More than that," Buck said. "Roy can run two hours one day."

"That's big?" she asked.

"Very big. Hundred times bigger than Roger Bannister's old four-minute mile at the time. If Roy wants it, it's his. A few years from now and hard work."

"The marathon's going to be big, Buck?"

"All he has to do is keep winning and bringing down the time. He'll make it. I've dreamed of two hours all my life."

"Roy knows about this?" Amy asked.

"Hey, I'm right next to you," Roy said. "Not down the street."

"He knows it," Buck said. "I've talked his ear off about it since he came to me as a kid."

"Do you believe it, Roy?" she asked, turning to him.

"Amy, let me run in a marathon first, okay?" Roy said.

"Roy's going to be big, Buck," Amy said. "Wait and see. They won't think of the marathon without thinking of Roy."

So it was. He kept winning, knocking down the time

from his first marathon of two hours, twelve minutes. Amy was relentless. She stayed in touch with the press, wangled a commercial and then two more as the marathon grew and Roy's name with it. They opened a running shop and had plans to open two more soon, were talking about the plans when they started out one morning for a light run.

They ran on the main highway for a few minutes, planning to turn off on to a smaller back road. Roy had never liked jogging on highways. There was something about runners that brought out violence in drivers. He had heard his share of taunts from passing cars, had heard stories from other runners who had had objects thrown at them and been buzzed by cars. Amy was running a few feet in front and to the left of him just off the highway. There wasn't much traffic, and they didn't hear the car bearing down on them.

Then there was a voice shrieking from the car window, a sudden *vroooom* ripping into the wind and a long blast on the horn. And then the blurred images: the chain whipping out and catching Amy around the waist, the hand on the chain and his wife being dragged ten yards, her head bouncing before the hand let go.

He picked her up in his arms, put her down, then walked around in circles. He moved into the middle of the highway, waving his hands and screaming as one car swerved around him and didn't stop. The next car, moving more slowly, didn't have a chance. Roy ran right in front of it, forced it to stop and pulled the driver out. He held her in his arms in the backseat of the car until they reached a hospital.

She had been long dead. The autopsy on Amy showed that she had suffered multiple fractures of the skull, a broken neck and pelvis. She was two months pregnant. The shock hammered down on him after the funeral. It drove him to Buck Lewis and his home in Colorado, where he took to bed and wouldn't leave it for days because of anxiety, and when he did he could hardly make it across the room. For the first time in his life he was afraid of the next minute, the next hour, of what would be there to rip his life in two again. Buck tried to bring him out of it; nothing worked.

"You're a loser, Roy, you know that?" Buck said suddenly one day after two months. They were sitting on the porch. Buck was drinking. He hadn't touched a drop in years, but now he was hitting the bottle heavily. His last track season was nearly over. They were moving him out after twenty-five years at the university. He had never been the beloved old man of the athletic department. He had fought too hard for his terrain, for his runners and the budget. He was not discreet, not politic. He had enemies. They said he was too old now.

"Since when?" Roy said, his face pale and his hands still with a slight tremble.

"Since you came out here to me," Buck said. "Since you began to feel sorry for yourself. Amy ought to see you now."

"What's that make you?" said Roy. "All you're doing is sitting around with your bottle and moaning inside about what's happened to you. You're out, Buck."

Buck stayed with a cool monotone. "She's a great excuse, isn't she? Feels kind of good inside, doesn't it? No more training. No more having to put yourself on the rack. No more plans. You've found your slot. Amy knew it. I always knew it. You got a little dog in you, Roy. We didn't keep after you, Amy and me, why, you'd roll right over on your back."

64

Angry, Roy stood up and pointed his finger at the bottle. "You're a lush, Buck. You're frying your brains." He walked to the door. "I'm going up to pack. I can't stand to look at you anymore."

Once more Roy felt oppressed by dread, first put there by Amy's death and left there forever by Oslo. Feeling the pendulum above him, he sat in the chair by the grimy window, looking down through the fire escape at the scruffy tree in the backyard.

Amy's death had marked the trail toward what would happen in Oslo. Leaving Buck in Colorado, Roy had flung himself into the marathon again, going faster and faster during that spree across Europe, where he had won four marathons in seven weeks, a grueling schedule. He had gone into Oslo only slightly worn at the edges but never more certain that he was on a beautiful roll with his talent and that the two-hour barrier was there now for the taking, if not in Oslo then soon after.

He kept reliving that race. It had seemed so perfect that day: weather, crowd, good field, the press from all over Europe expecting not just a new record but maybe marathon history. It was told, not a wisp of wind, and he knew he was going to run a time that no one else had ever done. He broke from the pack like a goddamn elephant with a cube of sugar on its back. He was over the first ten thousand meters in twenty-nine minutes and twenty-five seconds, and he couldn't have been blasted out of the groove with a land mine. But time is a ghost, changing shapes, calling you; then it's gone, and before you know it you are all by yourself and in a black hole.

Deeper and deeper into the hole, he lost his bearings and

all sense of time and body. Even so, he set a new world record of two hours five minutes; it was two minutes off his old record. And he knew that he might break the two-hour barrier in the next year. Though he was tired and a little shaken, he felt good inside. He'd taken the ghost into new spaces, and that was no small thing, because most runners were scared of time. And that was natural, he thought, because time meant more pain, going beyond what you knew you were as a runner and into dark waters.

Four hours after the race, he awoke with a start. It was dark outside. No lights in the room. But here he was looking at great, rolling waves of light on the wall. He blinked his eyes. They didn't go away. He turned on the room lights, and now the lights were dark and still rolling. His whole body was wet, even between his toes. He felt like he was melting. He rushed to the bathroom. He began to piss large clots of blood, then started to vomit black mucus, followed by black diarrhea. He crawled back to his bed, but he couldn't control the vomiting. He called down to the desk, and soon there was a group of men over him, watching him cry and moan and shake in his own vomit on the floor. "My God!" one of them yelled, and they took him to the hospital.

The doctors assured him he'd be all right. Stay on liquids, they said, don't get out of bed. But they didn't know what was wrong with him either. Back at the hotel, he began to tremble and sweat again, and once more the lights were there, flashing across the wall. The clots of blood kept coming; athletes urinate blood sometimes, but never like this. He tried to drift into sleep, was halfway there when he jumped up again, screaming, the bed wet with sweat and vomit. He felt as if he were having a breakdown. He looked into a mirror. His eyes were wild. He could feel the weight falling off his body. He was taken to another hospital. He went blank after a while. They had given him a sedative. He stayed there for a week; none of the doctors could diagnose what was wrong with him.

Back home in the States, he figured he would take five months off and begin running again. He was staying with his parents. He could still see his father trying to help him as he stumbled and screamed through the house in the middle of the night.

A couple of months passed, and then he was anxious to run again. He looked at his running shoes, looked at the land where he used to run as a kid, but he couldn't pull the trigger. He couldn't get out there and run. He started going into long silences around the house. And one night in a rage he threw all his running shoes out of the house and made a bonfire out of them. He didn't want to hear about running or marathons. Then, after another couple of months, he got an invitation to go to New Zealand for a ten-thousand-meter race, all expenses and then some.

With all his inner strength, he dragged himself to the high school gym and slowly began to build his body, then soon he was on the mechanical treadmill. He felt good. He was going to make it to New Zealand. He was going to start coming back. So there he was in Christchurch, New Zealand, the man who was king of the marathon, and the press was all over him and every local hotshot was waiting to take a piece of him. After all, they hadn't invited him over there to give him an award. They wanted to see him whipped.

But he got off real good. He stayed near the front, then built a lead with about nine hundred meters to go . . . and then they came. Three other runners shooting down the black, and everything quivering inside him. It was that moment when you want to win so badly, but as in all sports there's that flicker of aloneness and fear in you. There was just the sound of the spikes, the sound of spitting cinders, the breathing of the runners next to him, who sounded as if they'd had their throats cut. They weren't much—but he was less.

He was scared. His body seemed to be flecking off into pieces. He didn't want to win. He didn't want to be the best, not anymore, not ever. But still something in him was trying to hold on, and then suddenly he just turned off, dropped to his knees and sobbed into his cupped hands. The picture made the wire services. Soon it was all over the world that Roy Holt was through, that his burnout in Oslo had been real.

Maybe. But he knew this: He had run up against himself back there. He had run a hole through the wind in Oslo, and the stress of that pace had bent the metal in his mind. The quest for two hours had taken him somewhere that frightened him and he never wanted to go back to it again. Buck Lewis wasn't there to help him anymore.

But now, three years later, with Danny's help, he was slowly coming back. The tune-up races and that tough run in Ethiopia, he knew, had once more moved him toward the two-hour barrier—and the fear that began to drift up within him each new day.

He moved away from the window and went downstairs to meet Danny for their daily trip to the gym. If he had perceived anything by being around Danny, it was how easily men could delude themselves. The gym was loaded with failure, young and old fighters going nowhere but still holding tightly to the only dream left in their lives. They would do anything to keep that dream alive, from taking an endless series of five-hundred-dollar three-rounders to grueling sessions in the gym, and when they looked into the mirror they never saw ridges of scar tissue—only the dignity of an obscure but lifting purpose known only to them.

The gym, the proximity to such delusion and failure, had begun to weigh on Roy lately. Each time he taped a fighter's hands or sponged a battered face, he seemed to feel in some absurd communion with them, to see their dead ends as his own. Was he much better? he had begun to wonder. He had spent his whole life as a runner. The last thing he wanted to think of was a career. He had chased the two-hour barrier so long now that it was an extension of himself, and perhaps he, too, had lost touch with reality, like so many of Danny's fighters. He recalled Danny's words not long ago.

"You know," Roy had said, "a heavyweight fight, a good one, is a lot like a marathon."

" 'Cept you don't get hit runnin'," Danny said.

"I get hit," Roy said.

"Fighter gets hit too much, he gets a little bent up here." Danny pointed to his head. "Punchy. The world shrinks. Just four posts and canvas under his feet and a crowd always roarin' even when there ain't no crowd."

"I've seen some," Roy said. "They just talk too much. Their speech is slurred."

"When they quit," Danny said, "some of them miss gettin' hit. It's sexual with some of them. Seen some guys get hit so much they come in their jocks. So help me!"

"That's hard to believe."

"Ever see a guy start to melt under a big barrage? There's almost a look of . . . of . . . what's the word?"

"Ecstasy," Roy said.

"Yeah, that's it. They're hooked on pain. They like it. You like pain, Roy?"

Roy smiled. "You calling me punchy?"

"Naaaah," Danny said. "Just maybe they got another name for it in your game."

Going down the stairs, he wondered: Had his world truly shrunk to a couple of little rooms in Manhattan, a dreary gym and an obsessive dream that had twisted his life, had taken him so far from the ordinary routes of success for a young man? Was he irretrievably hooked on the search, the quest for something that was so elusive, so phantasmal that few—running critics or fans—took him seriously anymore, and every time he ran now there was a sense of pathos to the words written about him?

He shrugged the doubts from his mind. The country was full of play-the-pat-hand people. The death of Amy showed him that there were no pat hands in life. The barbarism of that day had brought him to his knees, had left him vulnerable and confused. The police hadn't given a damn; they'd just gone through the motions of an investigation. His father-in-law had blamed Roy, saying, "All this running. Why? For what? She only did it because of you. A stupid craze. I hope you live with this the rest of your life."

And he had—but not with stunting grief. Hardly a day passed that he did not think of her, and when he did it was with choking anger. He felt now that his life had been brutally violated and that he no longer knew who he was. He could only go forward toward the two-hour barrier, and there, within that exacting, cruel perimeter, he might find something that he could never lose, something that would allow him to live his life in peace again.

Roy skipped down the stairs to the front of the building.

Danny was sitting on the steps, watching an old man scream and rage at the sky.

"Look at that," Danny said. "Every day the same thing. I know his beef by heart."

"Is he drunk?" Roy asked.

"Naaaah," Danny said. "Life punches up people. That's all, ya know what I mean?"

"I'll be leaving soon, Danny," Roy said.

"Where?"

"Out to the desert," Roy said. "To work with Buck Lewis."

"Who's he?"

"Like you. Sort of a manager."

"Is he good?" Danny asked.

"The best," Roy said. "If he's sober."

5

Father Axel Dietrich, S.J., old-line Jesuit and scholar, tossed aside the sports section of *Asahi*, the picture of Kanji Sato still in his mind along with the two-column story. The murky world of *giri-ninjo*, he thought: death or the saving of face. The story was the first to deal with Kanji's planned two-hour attempt in the Boston Marathon a few months away; he had read a wire-service report out of Boston a week earlier that Roy Holt would be in that race for the first time in several years. He knew a little about Holt. He knew much about Kanji Sato, having been his private tutor since he was twelve and the man who had first sparked his interest in running.

With white hair, a leonine head and a body that few now could attach to a pole vault back in Germany, the priest was a foreign landmark in Japan. He was an Augustinian scholar, spoke five languages and had written many essays on the Japanese mentality, none of which had satisfied him. They were a people of groups who seemed impossible to group. But live over fifty years in Japan, and you could see *giri-ninjo*, death or the saving of face, begin to evolve; though the ethic had begun to fade with the Occupation, it was still never far beneath the surface of the Japanese character.

The *Asahi* story did not fool him. It was evasive, but Kanji's intention was there in so many sprinkled words: "ultimate . . . point of no return . . . spiritual mission . . . more than just a marathon." As the weeks passed, as the buildup grew, Kanji would become bolder, move closer to the fire, and although he would never dare use the word "seppuku," the public would know, and they would be watching and waiting for the history of a family to compress itself, then unravel on a single afternoon in faraway Boston.

He watched Ichy and Kanji make their way up the winding rock steps to the monastery. The priest considered his tactics. Evasion and then thrust? Or the direct plunge to the heart of his bizarre plan? A little of each, he guessed, but he warned himself to stay clear of what he believed to be the inherent evil of seppuku; good and evil were abstractions to the Japanese, especially to a young man who worshiped his ancestral samurai and was certain he had been given a divine mission. No, thought the Jesuit, he must use the marathon itself, Kanji's own weapon.

They left Ichy outside and went into Father Dietrich's study. The lights inside were a soft yellow, and the room smelled of stale pipe tobacco and old books. There was behind the big, worn desk, up on the wall, a painting of Saint Francis Xavier, the first Jesuit to come to Japan. The priest's swivel chair squeaked as he moved from side to side. A mangy old cat had come in the door and began to curl around Kanji's feet. The priest went over and picked him up, then carried him out of the study. The Japanese, he knew, were not overly fond of animals. Kanji broke the brief silence.

"So," Kanji said, "I suppose you've called me here for a touch, Father."

The Jesuit smiled. "America was not a complete loss. That is a nice bit of slang." He added: "We are not a begging order."

They both laughed. Kanji knew that the priest had never asked or accepted money from his family, other than for his services as a tutor. But Kanji's laugh was not lost on Father Dietrich. It was a short, nervous titter, the kind that often concealed deep emotion in the Japanese. If a maid dropped an expensive vase, or a man failed in an office duty, you would hear the same laugh. The priest guessed that Kanji knew why he was here and wanted to avoid any suggestion of a sermon. Besides, he was not very good at what the church called a sermon; his mind was too energetic for religious homilies.

"How well do I know the Japanese?" the Jesuit asked, playing with an old pipe bitten through at the stem.

"Father, the Japanese hardly know each other. They are tuned by an inner radar."

"Precisely," said the priest, tossing aside his pipe. "Do I have some of that radar?"

"I think not," said Kanji. "But . . . then again you've been here for over fifty years. Maybe."

"I think so."

"Shall I give you an examination?" said Kanji, smiling.

"Kanji-san," said the priest. "I have known you all your life. I know what you are up to."

"And what is that, Father?" asked Kanji, still smiling.

"You are preparing the stage for the act of seppuku."

"I'm afraid," Kanji said, unmoved, "that you have lived too long with your devious Jesuit mind."

"For you," interrupted the priest, "Boston is certain death. You cannot hope to succeed. We won't even talk about two hours."

"You forget the Hiroshima race," Kanji said.

"Do I know something about running events?" asked the priest.

"More than about the Japanese."

"Then listen. That time of two-zero-three is an illusion. Hiroshima is a flat, fast course. Faster and flatter than Fukuoka, if that's possible. You've never been on a rugged course like the one in Boston. It will smash you."

Father Dietrich knew the Japanese marathon men. They ran only one way, they came at you with the style of the coup, which the Japanese had made into a fine art in war and in life: the sudden, thrusting attack that gives no quarter, just brute offense, until they collapsed. The spectators knew what they were going to see at any marathon: speed, speed and more speed, and any man who stopped or took water was viewed as weak. They had had some success in Boston, and now he was listening to Kanji tell him a bit of history.

"Three Japanese, Father," said Kanji, "finished one, two, three in Boston one year. Another year, Shimoneki wired the field from start to finish. How rugged can it be? These runners were not even near my class."

"I don't know the caliber of those fields," said the priest. "For all I know, they could have been running against pandas. But I do know of one man who will be in Boston. You know of Roy Holt?"

"Certainly," said Kanji.

"I think you are a fine runner," said the priest. "Perhaps

even a great one in time. But let's look at the equation. You have a problem knee. Your two-zero-three is suspect. You will be in with Roy Holt on a tricky course with tough hills. Two hours is highly improbable. Can you really risk all, death by seppuku, against those kinds of odds? It is lunacy."

"Yes," said Kanji, rising, "because I know what I can do. And now I think I've heard enough."

"Sit down!" snapped Father Dietrich. "I have not finished." Kanji stayed on his feet.

"If I could," said the priest, "I would enter your mind and cut out your dark thoughts. But I can't. I can't stop you from going to Boston. Yet I must try to help." He slowly paced his study. "The Japanese can be an hysterical people. It is their Achilles heel. They go from calm to self-destructive emotion. Your only chance is to harness your emotion. Your emotion about your father has already taken you halfway to hell."

"Go on," Kanji said.

"Have you heard of *ki-ai?*" asked the priest. He was talking of the mysterious life force concentrated in the lower abdomen of the samurai. "Like most everything else, the samurai thought they owned it. But it can be developed by anyone, from a politician to a chess player."

Kanji's eyes lit up. "The samurai?"

"Yes, your beloved samurai." The priest thought of the father, Yatero, leering down at him. "Through the strength of mind that builds in the lower abdomen, a man can work with all the efficiency of a human bullet or sword."

"Can I . . . I mean is it possible that I could achieve it?"

The priest told him about a Zen monk in Kyoto. "If I send you to him, you must abide by his rules. He is a holy man. Lives in silence. Becomes the silence. You will have to leavy Ichy home. And go there immediately. There is no time to lose. It will not be easy."

The Jesuit sat down and began to write in Japanese. "I will give you a letter."

Father Dietrich finished writing and handed Kanji the letter. "Only one more word," the Jesuit said. "If you are so unfortunate as to go to Boston, remember this: you can't run in the past, you must run in the *now*. For yourself. If not, the past will kill you."

He walked Kanji to the monastery stairs, and as Kanji started down Father Dietrich grabbed Ichy's arm.

"Watch him in Boston," the Jesuit said.

The sumo wrestler did not have to ask what Father Dietrich meant.

6

Greta Overbeck lined up her girls and started to lead the last gym class of the day out of Central Park. Then she saw the two big men trying to hold on to their hats in the wind and walking toward her from Fifth Avenue. She had never known their real names and often got them mixed up, for they were both heavyset and jowly and looked the way her uncles had looked when she was a child in East Germany. Since her defection they had been of immense help to her, easing her transition and doubts. She could only tell them apart because one was an inch shorter than the other. They had told her to just call them the Smith Brothers, "like on the cough-drop box." The small joke had whizzed by her.

"We live and work out of New York," Big Smith said. "We're sort of unofficial greeters for people like you."

"And snoops," Little Smith had added.

"A link," said Big Smith, lacing his fingers. The translator had rattled on, and Big Smith said, "She getting all this?" The man nodded back.

"Yeah, well," said Little Smith, "anything she needs, any problem, tell her she should just call. Stay away from strange men. Get settled in. And if anybody bothers her, she should just call us right away. They blew a gasket over there in the East when she took off."

Greta started to speak in broken English, smiled, then went back to German. "She wants to know," said the translator, "for whom do you work?"

"Just tell her we're specialists," said Little Smith.

"Yeah," said Big, "we've handled them all. Ballet stars. Musicians. Film directors. Funny little guys back in the fifties with formulas in their heads who couldn't get across the street by themselves."

"But she's the prettiest one yet," said Little. "Tell her not to worry. Nobody eats you alive here. Anyway, not before six P.M."

So they trailed her loosely for six months, tapped her phone and planted a bug in her apartment as they tried to satisfy themselves that she was not Communist counterintelligence. Of course, you could never be sure; for it sometimes took years for a gambit to evolve. But Greta Overbeck, they knew, was not a good actress. After the early commotion of her defection, they could see that she was just a wife who was now far away from her husband. Often, they made visits to her place for a German meal. She was eager to know more about the country, and though they would never admit it, she had slowly lit a little flame in their lives; they always looked forward to seeing her.

Now the Smith Brothers joined her and walked with her out of the park.

"You're lucky," said Big Smith. "Fresh air. Outdoor work. Nothing like it."

"Beats sitting in a car half your life," said Little.

"I want to work in Washington," said Greta. Her English was still a little uncertain, but it was clear and fluent now.

"Soon," said Big Smith. "Give them time. Is that why you called us?"

"No," said Greta, "it is about my husband. Franz."

"Greta," Big Smith said, "there's nothing we can do. You know that."

"I can't live like this," she said.

Big Smith looked at his partner, then said to her, "If we could help you, you know we would. We like you, Greta."

Greta loped along, then said, "If I go to East Germany, what are my chances of getting out? I mean . . . with a new passport, the proper . . . what do you call it?"

"Cover," said Little.

"None and double none," said Big. "That's your chances."

"Forget it," said Little. "They'd have you in a minute. You weren't exactly the girl next door over there. People are always matching up faces."

"You'd need plastic surgery," said Big.

"Plastic surgery?" said Greta. "I did not think—"

"Are you crazy?" interrupted Little. "What the hell does this guy have?" He turned to Big Smith. "You should be so lucky."

"Greta, you, we . . . can't do a thing," said Big Smith. "Not as long as he's in Eastern Europe. He never goes anywhere else. You might have had a shot at him in Africa. But even that would have been tough. Nothing can be done. Unless he came here. First, he'd have to get here, then come over to us of his own accord."

"If I could only get there," said Greta.

"You're not going anywhere," said Little Smith.

"I see."

"No, you don't," said Big. "You made them look very bad. Go back, and nobody can help you. You'll be all by yourself, you understand? Chances are you'd never even see Franz. You'd just vanish."

They stood with her on the steps of the school, looking at the despair in her face. Big Smith grasped her hand and said, "Look, we'll think on it."

They left her and began walking down the street, then they started to trot when they saw a cop tagging their car. Big Smith flashed his identification. The cop looked at them from head to foot, then shook his head.

"What a job," said the cop. "The whole world's got a tit but me. How you guys ever get a job like that?"

"We learned to read," said Little. "You still got time."

They climbed into the car, and Little said, "I hope she doesn't try anything stupid. You can't ever find any form on blondes, you know. They're unpredictable."

"What do you know about blondes?" asked Big Smith grumpily.

"I've been around. Haven't been next to you all my life, have I?"

"Just most of it," Big Smith said.

"She goes back, she's gone."

"Greta's not stupid."

Big Smith moved the car out and said, "Tomorrow, we'll put a tap on her phone again . . . while she's at work."

Otto Albrecht knew Willy Schmidt well. He knew his charred talent. Never more than acceptable. As a five-thousand-meter man, he had been surpassed by the swift tide of youth always pushing up in the East German program. Albrecht knew of his muffled envy of Franz Overbeck. And mainly, he knew that Willy was a running derelict, hopelessly caught up in the atmosphere of the life.

Albrecht could have lopped off that life from Willy long ago, could have sent him to the factory where so many Willys before him had ended up. But Otto was not a rash man. He examined people, situations in detail, holding them up in the air like prisms, searching for the reflection that would best benefit Otto Albrecht—and East German athletics.

After Greta defected, Otto wanted to keep a close eye on Franz Overbeck. Was he depressed? Was he training properly? Was he trying to contact his wife? He wanted to get inside his mind, though he felt he knew that mind already. Overbeck would not falter. Psychological testing from the age of twelve showed that Franz's responses were rooted in one goal: running excellence. But Albrecht, who liked neatness and order, could not keep his mind off Franz and his wife. Hardly a romantic or even a man given to the most ordinary sentiment, he could not accept that any man could cut a woman like Greta out of his life without a regret that could turn into destructive longing and possible defection.

So, after the Greta affair, Albrecht called Willy to Leipzig. Willy expected the worst. "Swisssssssh!" he had said to Franz. "It is all over for Willy."

"Herr Schmidt," Albrecht had said, "I do not know you. I do not care about you. You are of no value to us as a runner. What should I do with you?" Willy started to answer, but Albrecht stopped him.

"How old are you?"

"I will be thirty-one," Willy said, almost wincing.

Albrecht spread his hands, palms up.

"You can do nothing. It costs the German Democratic Republic twenty thousand marks a year to keep you in the program. That is a high price for failure."

"I am grateful," said Willy, hearing the whine of machinery in some Leipzig factory.

"You like this life? It is healthy. There is—even for you —a modest recognition. There are privileges."

Eagerly, Willy said, "Whatever I can do."

"Franz Overbeck likes you, is that not so?"

"We talk."

"What does he talk about?"

"His training."

"Does he talk about his wife?"

"No, he never mentions her."

"Does he know where she is?"

"I don't think so, sir."

"From now on, you report back to me twice a month. Do you understand?"

Now, two years later, the shears still dangling over his lifeline to running, Willy was once more summoned to Leipzig.

"Did you know about this?" Willy read the letter Albrecht had handed him. It was a request from Franz. He was asking to represent East Germany in the Boston Marathon.

"I was going to tell you about it today," said Willy.

"You tell me nothing," said Albrecht.

"Because there is nothing, sir," Willy said.

Albrecht looked at the letter. "This is ridiculous. He must think we've lost our senses."

"I agree. I told him so."

"Then why? Boston is no challenge for him. There is nothing there for him. Is . . . is it that woman?"

83

Willy ignored the last part of the question and said, "Roy Holt will be there."

"Ahhhhh. I see. The American again."

Willy went on: "Franz believes that a major victory presents itself for the German Democratic Republic. Based on several things. We did not meet the Americans in Moscow —usually a great moment for us. And that Boston is very big in prestige. Highly visible."

Albrecht looked at him oddly. "I did not know you had such an analytical mind, Herr Schmidt. Go on."

"I don't," Willy said. "Those are Franz's words. He sees it this way. He could beat their best-known marathoner, Holt, in an event in which the Americans have come to believe they are superior."

"Who told them so?" Otto asked peevishly.

"Well, that's what they think."

"Their usual arrogance," said Albrecht.

"The Boston Marathon," said Willy, "is always a big news event. It's a showcase there. That and the New York Marathon."

"Is it on national television?"

"I'm not sure, sir," Willy said. Look at him, thought Willy, he's weighing the combinations; the buzzard's caught a scent.

Willy continued: "And there is one other thing. There is the course itself. It can be fast. Even better with a wind at your back. Franz sees a major breakthrough in time there. But he must have put all this in his letter, sir."

"Certainly," Albrecht said.

"And his request, sir?"

"I will not approve it," Albrecht said.

"Should I tell him?"

Albrecht tapped a pencil on his desk. He then swiveled

his chair around, leaving Willy to look at his long, stooped back; the back was always Otto's way of telling him that the meeting was over.

"Good-bye, sir," Willy said, once more relieved that he had not been fired.

"No!" said Albrecht, still turned away from him.

"What is that, sir?"

"Tell him nothing."

Willy left, and Albrecht sat there, holding up the prism. The husband of a defector, a beautiful defector, wants to go to America to run in a marathon that has national, even international, focus. The city is only four hundred miles from where his wife lives. The husband is the greatest marathoner in the world. He does not talk about her. He does not read her letters. He is dedicated. He obeys orders. He is a strong East German, still reaching to define himself in his event. What is in the balance? A certain victory that would have the impact of the Olympics here. Great recognition for the German Democratic Republic—and me. His only threat is a tattered American, Roy Holt. The only real danger: Greta Overbeck.

7

Buck Lewis's desert town was a row of mushy stone and weathered board. There was a gas pump, a supply store, a tired motel of twenty rooms and a bar with a busted neon sign. The town was a thin lifeline in Death Valley for lost tourists, prospectors who never ran out of prospects and desert rats like Buck Lewis. It was late afternoon, and the street was empty.

Roy looked at the motel first, then decided on the bar. Inside, there were a few dust-streaked beards talking softly in a corner, a bottle in the middle of their table. The rest of the place was made up of sticky tables, heat and a middle-aged barmaid with moist crusts of powder and rouge on her face.

"Beer," Roy said.

She brought him a beer, then moved over and slipped a quarter into the old jukebox. She stood there listening to the record, something about love lost on a Saturday night. The prospectors scowled at her.

Going behind the bar, she looked over at them and said, "Same to you!" She turned to Roy. "They hate the noise. Disturbs their whisperin' and dreamin' about all the uranium they're going to find. Fat chance!"

Roy found it hard to see Buck against this backdrop, so far from the insulated university life in Colorado. His mind reeled back to their first meeting. He had hitchhiked for days to see Buck Lewis. He had nothing going for him except his desire. He had been only adequate as a high-school miler, and a man of Buck Lewis's eaglelike stature in college running wouldn't even know he was alive. He hadn't written to Buck. He just showed up one day during the college's Christmas vacation. He could never forget the sight of Buck that day.

Roy had watched him from a distance for a half hour. Buck was out on the track, working with one runner; the rest were away for the holidays. The afternoon was cold, the track covered by a film of snow. Roy had eased his way finally over toward the track, and Buck started toward him. Roy heard only the snow crunching under his feet, and soon the eagle was next to him. He was short, wore a parka with the hood up, and his eyes were cold, almost harsh. He looked as if he had just descended from the pulpit of an ice church.

"Who're you?" Buck had snapped.

Roy explained his presence, apologized for his intrusion and nervously concluded a rundown of his high-school credentials, saying: "I wasn't much, I guess."

"That's the first thing you stop," Buck said.

"What's that?" Roy asked.

"Thinking you're not much. And thinking you're a miler. Everybody wants the mile. It's the glory run. Headlines and champagne. The ego express."

"Just give me a chance," Roy said.

"I like to take chances," Buck said. "If there's something to take a chance on."

Buck took Roy home to stay with him for the rest of the holidays. He lived alone in a house on a high hill, a fortress built of stone and wood over many years with his own hands. For two weeks he worked with Roy on the track, and he learned several things. He wasn't right for the mile. He took to the thin air of Colorado like a Sherpa. And his gait was close to poetry on the wind. Near the end, he had Roy blow out over five thousand meters. He liked what he saw. Roy had done the distance in thirteen minutes fifty seconds, and his kick was powerful at the finish.

"Nice," Buck said. "You'll get much stronger."

"You're going to take me?" Roy asked, excited.

"Forget the mile," Buck said. "The mile is drama. The sprint is drama. You're a distance man. Distance is art. It's the Tintoretto of running. But creating it is like a steady drop of water on your brain."

"You mean you really want me?"

"You got your chance," Buck replied.

It was more than a chance. Roy became Buck's private experiment. The old eagle seemed to sense that the kid might turn out to be his last champion. Aloof and moody, Buck had never been the most politic man on campus, and he was tolerated only because of his national persona and his ability to mold champions. He was a secret man, a remote legend. People could only wonder about him: why he had never married, why he was so unsociable and protective of his past.

"I never got a wife," Buck said once, " 'cause I'm not fit for any sensible woman."

Roy learned much more from him later. Buck had been

an ace bomber pilot, then a squadron commander during the war. After forty missions, the loss of friends, the bursting flak, the glinting yellow noses of German fighters, anxiety and guilt had smashed him to pieces. The war neuroses put him in a hospital in Europe. Once back home, he couldn't walk down a street or cross at a traffic light without breaking into a cold sweat and asking for help. Soon he never left his house; then his mother committed him to a veterans' hospital. He stayed a year.

"I beat it," Buck said. "But it took years. I just can't stand to be around people too much."

Roy had another beer and asked the barmaid, "Buck Lewis's supposed to meet me here. Has he been here?"

"He's over in the motel," the barmaid said. "Sleepin' one off. Comes in once a month and gets blind drunk. Nice old guy."

"Where's he live?"

"Straight out west. Little ghost town. Check all the shacks. He's got a Jeep out in front."

Roy walked over to the motel and got the key to Buck's room. The old man was sprawled on the floor. Roy searched his pockets for the Jeep keys, then slung him over his shoulder and carried him out to the Jeep.

They rode through the desert night for thirty miles until the moonlight showed him the town. Roy got out and looked up and down the street, listening to the wind rattle the broken windows. He was too tired to look for Buck's shack. He slung him back over his shoulder, kicked open the first door he came to. He put him down on the floor, then slumped into a corner himself. He listened to his mumbling and finally closed his own eyes.

A slant of sunlight cut through a window and woke Roy. He looked at his watch. It was nearly noon. Buck was gone. Roy jumped to his feet and walked outside. The sun was brutal. He squinted down the street, and he could make out the figure of Buck waving to him in front of a shack at the end of town. He drove the Jeep up to him. Buck's long hair was wet, his face a puff of white lather. He had cut off his beard and was now shaving the remains with a trembling hand.

"How you feel?" Roy asked.

"Don't talk," Buck said. "Sounds make me nervous."

He tossed Roy a pair of shears. "Give me a haircut. Doesn't have to be fancy."

"It won't be."

"Just clip. I'll tell you when to stop."

"You don't look like much," Roy said, beginning to snip away.

"Who does out here?" Buck said.

"You like it out here?"

"I've taken to the place like the buzzards."

"You in shape to start work soon?" Buck shook his head. "Hold still," Roy said.

"You don't need me," Buck said. "I told you that in the letter. You can train yourself. Runnin' ain't exactly Einstein's theory. No big secrets."

Roy kept on cutting. "I can't go it alone anymore. I need somebody who believes in me. You always said it could be done."

"That was a long time ago. The two-hour monster. Forget it, Roy."

"It's more than just two hours now," Roy said.

"What is it?" Buck asked, somewhat derisively. "Something for the memory of Amy? That's B-movie stuff."

Roy said, "She's just a shadow behind it. I don't know why I want it so badly. I just know I do."

"Go home," Buck said. "It's all over for us. Didn't you get the message in Oslo?"

"Buck, you're talking like you've died."

"I have. Since they gave me the boot back in Colorado. I'm now living a posthumous existence. Like you. After Amy."

Roy stopped cutting, and Buck got up from his chair. "You're right," Roy said.
Buck ducked his head in a tub of cool water and stayed under for a long minute. He came up gasping for breath. Roy threw him a towel.

"No, I'm not right," Buck said, squinting out of one eye. "You're too young for that kind of existence. You got to break out."

"I can. Just one more shot at the two. I can feel it. It's right there."

Buck thought a moment. "Okay, Roy," he said. "Beat the barrier or not. Just once more, ya hear me? Or your life won't be worth a grain of that desert sand. You can only run so long. You got to start livin' your life. A promise?"

"You're on," Roy said.

Buck pointed to a high dune out in the desert, saying, "Take a good look, Roy. See that devil? You're going to wish you never came out here."

8

The great bell of the temple pealed sundown into night.

Over a hundred Buddhist priests moved through the red-lacquered passageway leading into the temple. They were an explosion of color, wearing splendid canonicals of purple, scarlet or green with big hoods that fell behind their shaved heads. As they walked, they intoned in falsetto voices a chant, full of quivers and weird-toned trills. Incense curled up from a massive bronze brazier near the altar and rose in thick clouds as each priest cast on it a coarse powder of fragrant bark that had the scent of the lotus. Then there was only silence and smoke as thousands of pilgrims from all over Japan bowed their heads to the ground, and a single voice began to sing over them.

With the last blessing, Kanji raised his head and stared up at the giant center beam overhead, which nearly a century before had been lifted into place by thick ropes of human hair supplied by devoted women. He watched the priests and pilgrims move out of the temple. He asked one of the last monks where he could find a holy man named Rai. The monk nodded toward the altar. He looked and saw that it was the priest who had sung the benediction, the one in the orange robe who was easily six feet eight inches and had made him think of a giraffe. He walked up to the monk and stood in front of him. His hands on his knees, eyes straight ahead and legs straight back and under, Rai did not stir.

Kanji backed off and sat down well in front of him and to the side. The temple was still. The smoke from the brazier wiggled up behind Rai. There was an eerie silence that seemed to Kanji to come from the eyes of the monk, Mongolian and rapier, piercing and seeing nothing that could be of this world. He had seen many monks before, but never had he seen a monk—or any man—who was so impressive. He could only sit there and marvel at the sight, smiling inwardly at the world caricature that had every Japanese with buckteeth and thick glasses. He studied him closely. He was old, maybe sixty, yet there wasn't a crease, a line of age on his face; only his veined hands, long and thin and tapered at the nails, told of his age. He had big ears, a long neck and a posture that spoke of majesty.

After an hour, Rai moved. Kanji rose and moved quickly in front of him, handing him Father Dietrich's letter. Rai read it, looked at Kanji and said, "Come." The monk drew the hood up over his head, and they walked through the long passageway and then through a garden that was cold and dark and quiet, with only the sound of a nearby waterfall. They walked and walked, then walked some more, Kanji several lengths behind Rai's long stride. "What is ki-ai?" Kanji asked. The monk said nothing. Finally, they were at the bottom of a steep hill that led up to Mount Hiei, a Buddhist retreat northeast of Kyoto. They paused, and Kanji asked again: "What is ki-ai?" The hill was a half-mile long, and when they reached the top Kanji was limping.

Rai showed him to a two-mat room, then Rai left and came back with a bowl of rice and raw fish for Kanji, who was rubbing his knee.

"Is this where I will stay?" Kanji asked.

Rai nodded. "With me."

"My knee," Kanji said. "I can't seem to get it sound."

Rai said: "The Jesuit told." He bent over and began moving his long fingers over and around the knee.

"Explain *ki-ai*?" Kanji asked.

"*Ki-ai* is not words," Rai said.

"You do not talk much," Kanji said.

"There is more truth in silence."

"I would like to run in the afternoons. Then again some in the evening."

Rai shook his head. "When I say."

"I have to start training. Can I run soon?"

"We have much to do."

"In a week?"

"When I say," Rai said, then dropped back on his mat and quickly fell asleep.

Kanji watched the tall monk sleep. He would have to get used to this life, for he would be living here for three months. The irony of the course of events was not lost on him: a Jesuit sending him to an Eastern holy man to help him to master his weapon, the marathon, which was Western in origin and growth. The odd chain struck him as propitious, made him feel even more as if he was a man of destiny, someone with a mission that was pure and guarded by his ancestral gods. For this was no ordinary man to whom he had been delivered; he had learned a few facts about the priest before coming to Kyoto.

Rai was a *sennen*, and adept endowed with *jintsu-riki*, a divine power. From long bow to sword to judo, he was skilled in the ancient military arts, all of which were rooted in *ki-ai*. He was in his youth widely known for his defensive esoteric practices in judo. If he was on the scene he could heal cracked bone, stop the violent flow of blood from the nose and restore breathing after accidental strangulation. Still young and leaving the military arts behind him, except for the bow, he went into seclusion, staying alive by eating fruits, roots and the leaves of young plants. His skin grew whiter, his hair heavy and wild, giving the impression to the woodsmen that he had gone mad. When he returned home after a year, his family tried to divert him from his interests, but soon he was gone again, becoming a Zen monk and then going on to live in Tibet for three years.

Nobody ever learned what Rai took from those snowy mountain ranges. But when he returned, the tales of his magical senses were soon part of Japanese spiritual lore. Eyewitness reports abounded: the treelike monk knew no fatigue, felt no danger when scaling the most ominous of cliffs, knew neither heat nor cold and often exposed himself in meditation to the sun's rays for hours, and was once seen standing naked in a desolate woods for half a day during a blizzard. There was more. He could hear an ant creeping on the ground. He could correctly name the colors of the feathers of a small bird perched on a limb two hundred yards away; he could identify odors and hear voices long before his companions came upon them.

Kanji was eager to begin his work.

When he awoke in the morning, he found Rai standing and looking down at him, holding out the plain robe of a Zen novice and a pair of sandals. There was a bowl of rice on the floor next to the mat. "Is this all?" Kanji asked. Rai nodded. He waited for Kanji to finish eating, then said, "Come." They walked more miles into the woods behind the retreat, finally stopping at a stream. Kanji watched as Rai dug his hand into the brilliantly clear water. He saw the long fingers claw the black dirt from the stream's bottom. Holding two handfuls of earth, Rai told Kanji to lift the robe above his ailing knee. Rai then bent down and made a poultice of dirt for Kanji's knee. "Sit," said Rai. They sat and looked into the stream for over two hours. Kanji tried speaking, but Rai would not answer his questions. He gave up and just sat there, irritated at first, and then he became quiet inside. Several more hours passed before he was startled by Rai's voice.

"*Ki-ai* is the sun's energy," said Rai.

Fumbling for words, Kanji said, "I want that energy."

"If you listen." Rai turned his head to Kanji. "The ego is not the path to *ki-ai*. The mouth is not the path." From their first few minutes, Rai had been aware of Kanji's nature: very aggressive on the surface for a Japanese, who are outwardly docile and apologetic in their every action. Kanji fired more questions at him, but Rai said nothing. Kanji was aware of being reproved.

"Can we begin again?" Kanji asked. "What is *ki-ai?*"

"*Ki-ai* is the sun's energy."

"Is there a way to receive *ki-ai?*" he asked.

"By breathing in a new way," Rai said.

"How else?"

"By silence and the mind. By developing concentration. Ordinary man is like a samurai on a wild horse. The horse is mind. Unless samurai tames his horse they will never reach their destination."

"My concentration is good," Kanji said.

"Can you look at that rock"—Rai pointed to a small rock in the stream—"until morning comes?"

Kanji did not answer. Rai was pleased. He said, "Few men could."

Rai looked up at the sky. The afternoon was drawing to an end. "Come," he said. He told Kanji to climb up on his back; he did not want his poultice disturbed by walking. The two made their way down along the stream for a mile, then came to a hut that stood twenty yards from the water and was a hospice for wandering monks and pilgrims. It was always stocked with fruits and nuts and a small ration of rice. They stayed the night, and when morning came Rai once more made a fresh poultice from the stream's earth and put it on Kanji's knee.

"What does *ki* mean?" Rai asked.

"Mind," Kanji said.

"And *ai*?"

"To unite," Kanji said.

"Two words. Thus two minds. They must be united into one strong mind."

Rai went on to explain. *Ki-ai* was a three-pronged art: breathing, posture and the use of eyes. It was the art of fixing one's mental energy upon a single object with the determination to achieve or subdue that object. *Ki-ai* was a power source, generated by breathing; its center was the *tanden*, or lower abdomen. When a warrior or citizen had *ki-ai*, he acted without design, without idea or mind, exploded into a dynamic energy against his enemy or toward his goal. Rai, speaking carefully and slowly, thought of war history to illustrate his point: the Japanese love of the coup and the attack on Pearl Harbor were group reflections of *ki-ai*, in a way; the sudden, fearful expulsion of mass energy against a target. But he hated war and blood and wan ton death. He knew it would strike recognition in Kanji; Rai declined to use war as an illustration.

Kanji nodded, asking, "Will all this help me in the marathon?"

"What is a marathon?" Rai asked.

"A distance that I must run."

"Why?"

"For honor."

"Whose?"

"My grandfather's. My father's."

"And if you do not succeed?"

"I prefer not to think of it," Kanji said, looking away from Rai's eyes.

"*Ki-ai* is life," Rai said. "Not death."

"Shame lives with me."

"The only shame is a wrong death."

"Can *ki-ai* deliver this goal?"

"How fast must you run this marathon?"

"Faster than people say is possible."

"Does the marathon have a point of attack?"

"The miles."

"It has no eyes. No heart. No mind. No body. It is a powerful foe."

"Yes."

"For then it must live in the mind of the man who runs it, and it must be beaten there."

Kanji started to speak, but Rai raised his long finger to his lips.

Rai talked on quietly. *Ki-ai*, he said, was and could be a lethal force for good, for personal self-attainment; it was like a new source of fuel for the world, only this was energy for the individual. Every human being who ever lived had had it, and most died not even knowing. *Ki-ai* was in every person, scattered, diffuse, and left to burn out uncontrolled. The first step in attaining *ki-ai* was to know that there was such energy. The second was to gather it up, to bring it into one place where it could be worked on, felt and used readily.

For the assembling of the energy, deep breathing was the primary drill. Rai took a piece of six-foot long cloth and folded it twice, then passed it twice around Kanji's stomach just below the lower ribs. He then told him to inhale the air deep into his stomach, to keep his body loose, to hold his shoulders down, his trunk bent forward. The posture stimulates the blood, invigorates the muscles and the organs.

"All men," Rai said, "can be judged by their eyes. When one's mind is dark the eyes are dull. Hear a man speak and look at his eyes. He cannot conceal the secrets of his soul. The eyes are mirrors." Rai rose. "Do you understand?"

"I will leave now," he said. "I will be back soon."

"When?" Kanji asked. "What shall I do here?"

Rai said, "Breathe the way I have shown. Sit. Watch. Listen to the wind. Listen to the silence."

Two days passed, and they were the longest in Kanji's life. The stream in front of the hut became putrescent to his nose, vile to his eyes. The silence hammered in his ears. He despised Rai, held himself in contempt for having listened to the musings of a man who knew nothing of the real world, for having submitted to a mumbo jumbo that seemed so far from Boston and the marathon. What was Roy Holt doing now? He began talking to himself. Running, that's what you're doing, Roy. That's sensible. Runners run. You're not sitting here staring at a stream and gnawing on nuts like a chipmunk.

By the end of the fourth day, he stopped resisting and began to breathe deeply the way the monk had shown him, shouting on inhalation and sucking the air far into his *tanden*, working on his posture each time. By the end of seven more days, he could breathe Rai's way two thousand times a day, and the stream became clear and clean again, and for several flashing moments he saw things as if he were the first man on earth.

Two weeks passed in all, and then Rai returned. Kanji was sitting by the stream, breathing rhythmically, his eyes steady on the rock. Rai bent down and moved his fingers over Kanji's knee. He looked into his eyes and was pleased with the brightness.

"You will run now," Rai said. "Your knee will not pain you anymore."

"I feel different," Kanji said.

Rai began to walk. "We shall talk now only a few words once a week. When you run, keep your chin tucked well into your neck, your nose in line with your navel, your ears in line with your shoulders. Your mind on your *tanden*."

They lived at Rai's room in the Mount Hiei retreat, and each day was the same: the breathing exercises in the morning, two sessions of running in the afternoon and early evening, and several hours at night in the garden by himself. They did not speak to each other, but always when they were in their room, getting ready to sleep, Kanji seemed to feel an energy coming from the monk. Four weeks went by, and the miles were bending under his feet. There seemed to be a lightness to his body, a sense of power that he could feel in each muscle. He was certain that *ki-ai* was within him.

"I have *ki-ai*," Kanji said one night, when he had been allowed to speak.

Rai did not question him. Getting up, he said to Kanji, "Come." They walked to the kitchen of the monastery, and Rai stood in front of the stove. The working monks stopped what they were doing and seemed to be frozen into position, their heads turned toward Rai and Kanji. Rai waved his hand, and every monk knew what he wanted. One of them brought him a poker. He held the poker in front of his eyes for long minutes, then dropped it into the flame of the old stove and kept his eyes on the end that was sticking out.

After twenty minutes he waved to a monk, who, wearing a heavy glove on his hand, pulled the poker out of the fire. The monk then held it out at the level of Rai's lower abdomen. The front end of the poker was red and smoking. He motioned for the monk to put it back. And then Kanji saw, felt a strange force gathering. Rai was standing there, both thumbs of his hands squeezed tightly under his fingers, his long legs pressed to the floor as if they were a conductor of power. He gave a short nod for the monk to withdraw the poker and place it in front of him again.

Nobody moved in the kitchen. Kanji began to sweat, but there was not a drop on Rai's face. The great priest fixed his eyes on the red poker end, drilled his legs deeper into the floor, tightened the fingers on his thumbs, then breathed deeply and sharply ten times. And on the eleventh inhalation, there was a shattering, bloodcurdling burst of sound from Rai's mouth, sending his right hand out and firmly on the poker, wrapped there for all to see. The hand stayed on the poker for ten seconds. Kanji could smell the flesh burning, so intense was his reaction to what he was seeing.

Finally, Rai withdrew his hand and opened it for Kanji and all the monks to see, causing a shuddering expiration of breath among them. Kanji could not believe what he saw.

Rai's hand was smooth, the color of bamboo that it had always been, not burned or charred or dripping fluid from horrible burns that should have been there—not even red. Rai was not even rubbing his hand. He simply told the monk to put the poker back into the stove.

"That is *ki-ai*," said the assistant, looking at Kanji.

Rai looked at Kanji now, then at the poker. Once more he nodded to the assistant to get the poker. He held it up, and Rai motioned with his eyes for him to put it in front of Kanji, who flinched and stepped back, then, seeing all the eyes on him, moved toward it. Rai studied him closely. Kanji moved his eyes between the poker and Rai, trying to gather force from him, trying to accumulate courage inside himself. The sweat poured off his forehead. He started to move his hand out dumbly, knowing that that was not the way. He tried to fasten himself to the floor. And then he began his breathing. Once. Twice. His eyes stayed on the steaming poker. He could feel the palm of his hand on fire, the searing rise of pain and the cracking of flesh. Six times. Nine. Ten. He inhaled and then tried to pull the sound from his *tanden*, tried to free the energy, but nothing happened. His hand shot out, felt the heat of the poker. Rai's own hand moved up and then fell back to his side. Kanji's hand did not attack the poker; the tension melted among the monks.

"I have no courage," Kanji said, the front of his robe wet with sweat.

"*Ki-ai* is not courage," Rai said, knowing that he would never have allowed Kanji to grab the poker, knowing that this was not a test for a novice. He had only wanted to show him the force of *ki-ai*—and humility.

"I will never have it," Kanji said, still looking at the poker which was now on top of the stove.

Kanji raised Rai's right palm in his hand and looked at it.

"Nothing," Kanji said.

"There is time," said Rai.

All the monks bowed as Rai strode from the room.

9

Willy Schmidt kept his mind on his work: Franz Overbeck, who was now moving up a wooded slope of morning
light and shadow. Willy lagged behind, sometimes running
in place, trying to give Franz room and still not lose him.
Usually, they took these light runs together once or twice a
week before Franz's heavy afternoon training, when all the
Institute's technology seemed to trail behind him. But Franz
hadn't asked him lately, so Willy, worried that something
might be going on that he didn't know about, had waited
for him this morning and followed.

Franz moved over the top of the slope, and Willy jogged
up it cautiously. When he reached the end of his climb, he
looked down at a rocky ravine. His eyes searched quickly
for Franz. Willy couldn't pick him out. He was about to go
down, thinking Franz was already running up the hills leading out of the ravine. Suddenly he dropped to the ground,
out of Franz's sight.

The scene puzzled Willy. His friend was just squatting

down below, motionless, his head lifted to a jutting slab of rock where a large, regal elk stood imperviously above him, its tall antlers catching the sparkle of the sun.

Later in the afternoon, Willy watched the line of vehicles move out slowly behind Franz on the road below the camp. There were the usual ambulance and Mueller's car, but now there was a portable lab in a van. The lab never went out Willy knew, unless Franz was preparing for a big race, and this was the first day for the lab; something was going on.

Willy hopped on his bike and took a short cut through the woods, where he could get a good view. The path would lead him to a summit above the road and bring him out a couple of miles ahead of Franz. He got there well in time and waited for twenty minutes, and finally Franz broke into sight, the vehicles behind him.

Franz was on an open stretch of road, about four hundred yards away, when he began to gun into a long speed interval, his body hitting the wind like the edge of a knife. What a sight, thought Willy. Franz and the vehicles stopped roughly fifty yards away from Willy, who then watched the technicians go to work, flurrying around Franz. One of the men looked at his stopwatch, nodded and patted Franz on the back.

The scene was familiar. They took some blood from Franz's earlobe to measure his lactic acid buildup, which can wreck a runner's body quickly in a race and is also used to assess the rate at which he burns sugar. Franz removed the spirometer from his mouth, the snorkellike device that gauged the volume of oxygen in his lungs. Then they all walked back to the lab, where they would study the ECG monitor that was hooked up to Franz's chest.

He waited, then watched Franz and the group start off again down the road. Willy jumped on his bike and raced back to the camp.

There must be something here, thought Willy. There has to be. His orders had been painfully clear when Albrecht had called him in two weeks before. The director, his patron, wanted him to watch Overbeck more closely than ever, and he wanted his room searched. "If he even has one of her old hairpins," Albrecht said, "I want to know it." Albrecht had been petulant, even truculent. "Do I make myself clear, Schmidt?" he snapped. Yes, yes, thought Willy, as he now eased through Overbeck's quarters up at the training camp, but I can't find one scrap of her continuing existence in his life.

Slowly, carefully, he searched the room. He lifted up the mattress, burrowed into every corner of his closet. Nothing. He came across a small safety deposit box. Locked. Willy thought of smashing it open, then changed his mind. He felt guilty. It was one thing sticking to Franz like a fly, quite another to intrude upon whatever secrets he might have. But I am desperate, Franz, Willy thought. You have never been desperate. It has all been so easy for you: the natural ability and physiology, and all that meticulous attention paid to it. I have to look out for Willy. It's the only life I know, Franz.

He had been in the room for over an hour when he went back to the bed once more. He picked up the pillow and poked absently inside the pillowcase. He pulled out the paper and glanced at it quickly. It was a half-composed letter to his wife, Greta, dated only two days before. He heard the door of the cabin being opened. He jammed the letter into his pocket. Footsteps in the outer room. Willy swallowed hard; he did not move. Then he heard the voice call out. "Franz! You here? Franz!" It was Uncle Heinrich. The shoes creaked nearer to the bedroom. Willy thought of hiding under the bed. The knob turned on the door. Willy drew a long breath.

"Willy!" Heinrich shouted. "Willy! I do not believe this!"

"I . . . I . . ." Willy gave up. He knew an explanation was useless.

"What did you find, Willy!"

Willy, like a frightened bird leaving its branch, darted past the uncle. Heinrich, tumbling against the wall, caught him by the shoulder, halted his stride for a second, and then Willy was gone. Once out of the house, he ran until he was out of breath. He sat down under a tree, read the letter, then went to the administration building to call Albrecht.

They go about it all with a grim tenacity, like an old Münchener viewing his spaetzle or his stein of beer, thought Albrecht. Eating and drinking there is serious business, and so is hunting in East Germany. There is no air of sport, of leisure, just killing by assembly line or computer. First, there is the bugle, the noise of the beaters, the sudden panic of thousands of hares felt in the woods, and then the perfectly timed explosion of guns sending a gray mist of smoke up and through the bare trees.

Albrecht was not at ease here in the woods north of Berlin. But he had to be there; he wanted to close a deal, a fact that made him no different from a salesman eyeing a contract on a golf course in the West. He had been invited by Joachim Krueger, number three man in the Sports Federation. This was a political outing, and if Albrecht was pleased it was with good reason. Obviously, important people had their eyes on him. This was not a place for party hacks, or the usual government careerist.

Albrecht felt awkward drawing his weapon along with the twenty other dignitaries in the lodge. Few of them knew what to do with a gun. They were there for the show, for the exposure, while twenty others—farmers mainly—drew the guns that would thin out the hare population. No one brought their own guns, for owning one was illegal in East Germany. Only the East German leader, President Koenig, who stepped out of a limousine near the shack, did not have to check out a rifle. His was in a black case carried by a gun bearer.

The woods were cold and silent, except for the squawks of birds and the murmurs of men talking in small groups. Albrecht blew breath into his cupped hand, then gripped his rifles tightly. He hoped that he would not have to see one of the dead hares; he hated the sight of blood. But, he had to admit, they were a pleasure to eat. He was clearly out of his element, he thought. He did not like traveling, was not fond of the countryside. He was never more secure than when he was behind his desk, where he could be in control, reduce his vulnerability to the unexpected.

In full hunting regalia, the President strode toward the lodge, greeting the others with a tired wave of the hand, his belly marching out in front of him to the dissonant clapping of the crowd. Here was power, thought Albrecht, looking at the old President in leather pants, high boots, Tyrolean hat. They would shoot, they would eat, and they would talk; he hoped the President would say something to him.

"He is getting old," Krueger said, standing next to Albrecht. "He has been a great man. He is not a Moscow cutout. He has made, created, his own communism here."

"Yes, a great man," Albrecht said. He was wondering what he would say to the President over lunch at the lodge.

"All this is his work," Krueger said. "Before, they used to slaughter the animals like they do now in the sick West. Our killing is much more democratic. It gives only those with talent and interest a chance to hunt. Income and position do not matter. All these people belong to hunting societies. They must pass tests to become members. Then they must work as well as shoot. Feed the game in bad winters. Keep the woods in order. Control the vermin. A finely tuned organization."

"Like our Sports Federation," Albrecht said, not missing a chance to commend Krueger. "You have it tuned to perfection."

"Nobody can just go off and hunt on his own," Krueger said. "That is why you are here."

"I do not quite . . ."

The bugle ricocheted through the quiet woods, calling the hunters to their positions. "Later," Krueger said.

Albrecht took his position in the circle that spread out in front of the hundred beaters. Slowly, over a mile, the circle drew tighter and tighter, and the noise increased. The strategy was to drive the hares to the ones who would use their guns. And now they came, swarms of brown, leaping, zigzagging, frightened animals. The politicians only lifted their guns as if they were getting ready to fire. The hand cameras of the television crews panned down the line of politicians and then stayed on President Koenig, who ceremoniously raised his gun to position under his heavy jowls, aimed and fired, sending his hare bounding on weak legs and then tumbling head over heels, as if in slow motion, to a frozen position at the base of a tree. Everyone clapped. The President then signaled the marksmen to his left to begin their work.

The woods echoed with rifle blasts for nearly a half hour. The noise, the smell of cordite, the smoke curling up among the trees—all of it made Albrecht want to clasp his ears, put a handkerchief to his eyes and nose. He did nothing. And then there was quiet as the circle drew very tight around the clumps of hares, bleeding and rigid, strewn before them. The President began walking back toward the lodge, having congratulated the marksmen. They had bagged fifty hares. "Not a bad first kettle," said the President. "I know you will do better next time. We'd like about two hundred on this hunt, men." The hunters would shoot until dark.

"You know," Krueger said, "I could not help but think of the hares. Such easy victims. The noise. It drives them right into the circle. Why do they always run into the circle? Why not away from it?"

Albrecht knew nothing about hunting or the habits of animals. But he thought he should say something. "I guess, Herr Krueger, they follow the leaders."

"Precisely, Herr Albrecht," Krueger replied. "Well said. They follow the leaders. It is much the same with our problem."

"You mean, of course, the Boston Marathon."

"Yes. It bothers me, it and Overbeck. Why? Why? I believe he is just following the leaders. The Japanese. And the American. I do not like it."

"I cannot deny it. It is a personal thing with him."

They were walking now about fifteen yards behind the President. Koenig was getting ready to climb over a felled tree in his path. His aides started to help him, and he quickly brushed them away.

"You see," Krueger said, watching President Koenig straddle the tree, "that is a very proud old man. He loves to make the West look bad. On the other hand, the endless defections over the Wall make him look bad. It is, you see, largely a battle of propaganda, of wits." Albrecht resented being talked to like a young trainee; he knew the contours of the battle.

"The Federation is a principal weapon," Krueger went on. "With it, his athletes, he has made the West, especially America, look quite silly. Imagine. East Germany, which could fit into one of their states, embarrasses America on the playing field. It is a source of great pride to him."

"Well, Herr Krueger, that is the point that I submit to you. The propaganda value is great. And I have no doubt that Overbeck will win. And who and what will be beat? He will beat the celebrity American on his own course. He has won it three times. He will beat the Japanese, who has been so much talked about of late. It is an easy course. A great magnet of publicity. I believe Overbeck might come up with his fastest time. I have studied the combinations. They suit me."

"I have taken this up with the committee," Krueger said. "They do not like it. They do not see the international value. The gain."

"And you, sir?"

"Of course, I see the value. It all looks so easy. That is what worries me. It is like shooting hares."

"Easier," Albrecht said. "You know I am conservative by nature. I have studied the matter."

"You are an ambitious man, Herr Albrecht."

"Only for the country."

"You are no fool. You know what is at stake."

"You mean his wife. It is a gamble only on paper, Herr Krueger. Overbeck has no interest in her."

"You may be right. But if he went over, you can imagine the blow to us. I shudder to think about it."

"It will not happen."

"And then there are the expenses. For two weeks. Overbeck, so many security men. They will have to be top line. . . ."

"I have your authorization, then?"

"Most certainly not. It is your decision. It is your department. The committee is split down the middle on this decision."

Albrecht knew what that meant. The six members of the Federation's hierarchy knew how to cover themselves; they were experts in survival. They wanted the trumpet of Boston to blow over East Germany and their careers, yet they had not risen in the government machinery by ignoring the down side of life; they would play, but quietly. If Albrecht did send Overbeck and . . . He did not want to think of it. viewed with indifference, that he would be seen as an administrator who could not seize the moment; from then on, there would be no damage to his career, only inertia. If he did send Overbeck and . . . He did not want to think of it. Intractable. Ambitious. Selfish. Reckless. These would be the words that would be used against him.

"And your decision, Otto?" Krueger asked, bending down and examining one of the hares.

"I will make it soon," Albrecht said.

They stood in front of the lodge, waiting for the morning's kettle to be lined up in front of them. The gamekeepers dropped the hares down neatly in a row. The blood was sticky on their furs, their eyes glassy.

112

Krueger lifted a hare by its ears. He held it up in the air, letting the blood drip out of it. Smiling, he said, "Keep in mind only this, my ambitious Otto. Nobody hunts alone." He dropped the hare.

"You like sour hare?" Krueger asked, walking toward the lodge porch.

"Yes, it is a delicacy. I could use some lunch."

"Oh, I am very sorry, Otto. The lunch will only be for ten of us. Some very private matters to be discussed. You understand."

"I do," Albrecht said curtly.

Sitting in the chair in front of Albrecht, Willy fingered the letter in his pocket, his ticket to his small place in the program. By now, he knew the letter's content by memory. There was no doubt that Franz still loved Greta. He told her that he was trying to go to Boston. He would be stopping in New York for two nights; nothing could keep him from her. Willy had something that Albrecht would dearly pay for; now Willy could play the tune for the cadaver behind the desk. He watched Albrecht tap his pencil-thin fingers anxiously on its surface. Pick the right moment, Willy, he thought. Stay in control.

"Well, well," Albrecht said impatiently. "Your report? I do not have all day."

"I watched him closely for two weeks, sir," Willy said.

"Get to the point, Schmidt."

"You know he runs in the afternoons. The ambulance follows behind him. They stop. They take tests of his blood periodically."

"Schmidt, I know all this. What are you telling me! That is standard procedure. I didn't send you there as an observer. You are telling me nothing, you fool!"

"But you don't know that he also runs in the morning. Very early. By himself. I followed well behind on several mornings."

"And so?"

"He runs for four miles. And then he stops. The same place every morning."

"And ?"

"He squats and looks up at an elk, a huge elk standing up on a high rock. He squats there for fifteen minutes. Just looking up."

"There are no elks in East Germany."

"There's one up there. A big one. I've seen it with my own eyes."

"No elks, Schmidt. Are you trying to make a fool of me?"

"No, sir. Psychologically, there may be something of value to you. Why would a man run to the same spot and stare up at an elk?"

"I am not interested in elks. Nor red deer." He tapped his fingers swiftly now. "Nor hares. You know what I want."

"His uncle found me in the bedroom," said Willy. He could hear his words jetting out, then slamming back into his face. He had just made a terrible error, he knew. He had just admitted that he had been exposed, that he could not be of any more use to him. Why? Goddamn it, Willy, why!

"I see," Albrecht said, rising from behind his desk. "And what did he say?"

"Nothing. I ran out of the room." Willy dug his fingernails into the letter in his pocket; it was now or never.

Albrecht circled the desk and moved in back of him. "So you have found nothing. I am relieved." Willy could not believe the words. He was being released from the necessity of betraying Franz; he had never wanted to do that to Franz, to destroy all his plans for Boston. Franz had never ignored him; he had looked out for him, made him a colleague, while all the other runners wondered why.

"Yes, I must say I feel better," Albrecht said. "I did not want to lose the advantage of Boston. I think we will grant his request for Boston."

Willy sighed. Albrecht kept walking in back of him, the squeak of his shoes drawing closer and closer, until he felt two sharp pats on his shoulder. Albrecht then walked quickly back to his desk chair.

"So it is over now, Willy. You have watched Franz all these years. And found nothing. You have done well. But now, I must say that it is over."

"You mean, sir, that I do not have to spy on Franz anymore?"

"Yes, Willy." He swiveled in his chair, turning his back once more to Willy. "And I am afraid that you are no longer in the program."

"But, sir!" Willy felt his stomach drop, his knees quiver.

"I am sorry. You are of no more use. The uncle has surely told Franz of your presence in his room."

"Yes . . . but . . . maybe I can work here at the Institute in some way."

"You were never much of a runner. I daresay you would be worse as a trainer."

"I'll do anything," Willy said, talking to Albrecht's back. "Anything. Just please let me stay with the program. You have the power to do that, sir."

"There is no room for hangers-on, Schmidt. Every cent we spend must count. I cannot afford you. That is the fact."

"Just like that," Willy said. "My whole life."

"Do not be sentimental, Herr Schmidt. I will see that you get a job in a factory."

Willy thought of dark interiors, of noise and the smell of machinery and walls that closed in on him. No more sunlight, no more hills, no more the sweet feeling of sweat breaking through his skin. He felt dazed, lost, cut off from the only family that he had ever known.

"It was like a family to me. You know I was an orphan."

"We all have to make our way," Albrecht said.

Now he knew he must use the letter. "All right," he said, "but you will never know about him, will you? I know. You would like to know what I have?"

Albrecht spun around in his chair. He gauged Willy's face, looked for the truth behind the words; he saw nothing. If he had had information, he would have played it earlier to insure his place in the program. The man, after all, thought Albrecht, was an informer and a coward. That kind of man did not play games. He was bluffing, a poor, helpless bluffer, that was all. There was only panic on Schmidt's face. "It is useless, Herr Schmidt," Albrecht said. "There is no information."

"You will see," Willy said. He started to reach into his pocket, but he could not do it, could not toss the evidence on his desk. The letter might save him for a while, but that was all. Albrecht would hate him for showing the letter. He wanted Boston as much as Overbeck! Willy's position was clear. There was no way out. There was no desire for revenge on Albrecht, nor a malicious envy of Franz to motivate him. It would be without purpose; he had only wanted to save a spot of sunlight for himself. That, he could see, was gone now.

"You reach into your pocket," Albrecht said, smiling, "but there is nothing, Willy. Just your sweaty hands."

"You will know one day," Willy said.

"That will be all, Schmidt." Albrecht waved him out rudely.

That night, drinking heavily, Willy decided to call Franz up at the camp. He waited for Franz to come to the administration building to answer the phone. He gulped down a shot of vodka as he heard him speak. "Hello!"

Wiping his mouth nervously, he said, "Franz, it's me— Willy." Franz said nothing.

"Franz, it's me. I'm sorry." There was just the hum of the line.

"Franz, I didn't tell him! I didn't tell him about the letter! He knows nothing. He is going to let you go to Boston, Franz!" The hum continued.

"Franz, listen to me. I loved you, Franz! I was only trying—"

He heard the click, then the long, droning buzz on the other end of the line. "It was all I had," Willy said, dropping the phone to his feet.

Two days later they found Willy in a stolen government car punched violently into a tree up in the Harz Mountains, his head hanging half off.

The autopsy showed that he had been drinking heavily. His death was ruled an accident. Unofficially, it was widely thought that the car had been driven directly, with purpose, into the tree.

Franz did not go to the funeral; nobody did.

10

"Not a chance, young lady," said the doctor, guiding her to his entrance on Park Avenue, "You are either crazy or totally innocent. Although you don't seem crazy to me."

"I have a good reason, believe me, Doctor," said Greta.

"No reason would be good enough," said the doctor.

"Will you at least listen?" asked Greta.

"I don't want to know. I'm a sucker for a good story."

"But . . ."

"Good day, my dear. I should say I'm sorry, but I'm not."

Greta left the office, having been with the doctor only ten minutes. Little Smith and Big Smith sat in their car and watched her lope down the street. Little Smith had once estimated that they had spent two thousand hours of their lives waiting in a car somewhere; they were what is known as "tail specialists." With the State Department for fifteen years, they had looked at more back fenders than a garage mechanic while following foreign diplomats, minor and major, and defectors who might be plants. It was dull, plodding work, but not without its compensations. They ate in good restaurants, slept in quality hotels, and seldom saw their wives. "That's a perk if ever there was one," Little Smith often said. But mostly their lives had been spent on quiet streets and in dark cars. They were on this street, this day, because of Greta. They had reported their concern about Greta, her state of mind, back in Washington. Nobody there wanted Greta back in East Germany.

"Let's go," said Big Smith. "We can pick her up later."

"She's probably only got a cold," said Little Smith.

"She goes to a Park Avenue doc for a cold?"

"You know how women are. They look for doctors like they look for boutiques."

"What's those letters here behind this guy's name?" asked Big Smith.

"Some kind of specialist, I guess."

"Let's find out."

The doctor was still in the reception office; they flipped out their identification.

"The girl, Doc," said Big Smith. "What'd she want?"

"You see," said the doctor. "I knew she was trouble." The doctor was talking to his nurse. "Come on into my office."

"Just routine," said Little Smith, sitting down. Big Smith stood, looking around at the diplomas.

"I'd never touch a face like that, gentlemen," said the doctor.

"You a plastic surgeon?" asked Big Smith.

"Yes. What has she done? Why did she want to change her face?"

"You mean, she wanted you to do some cutting?" asked Big Smith.

"Can you believe that!" said Little, looking at his partner.

"Yes," said the doctor. "But believe me, gentlemen, I do not do that sort of thing. Sure, I do some cosmetic work. But mostly rich old women, or actresses and actors who cannot bear aging. But this girl—it would be defilement. What could make somebody so desperate?"

" 'That sort of thing,' you said," said Big Smith. "You mean she could possibly get it done somewhere else? No questions?"

"Sure," said the doctor. "You can get anything in this city. It would probably cost her about three thousand dollars. It's a minor job. The wrong man with the knife could screw that face up."

"How would she find such a guy?" asked Little.

"Just look in the personal columns of the papers. They run ads. They watch their language. Usually it's something like 'Cosmetic Consultant, low-cost and painless. Change your look.' That sort of thing. They don't say too much. They're careful. Most of them, you see, have lost their license to practice."

Little looked at his partner. "She thinks a new face will get her back into East Germany. She thinks she could talk Franz out of there."

"Would there be a big change?" asked Big Smith.

"Around the eyes, no," the doctor said. "Her nose would have to be broken for dramatic change."

Big Smith thanked him and started to leave, saying, "Shit. A broken nose. Her nose."

The doctor looked up. "That's nothing. You want to see some pictures? I'll show you a nose that fell off. I'll show you breasts that swelled to zeppelins and dripped with pus."

"Give me a break, Doc," said Big. "I'm going to lunch."

"Hog butchers," grumbled the doctor, turning back to the papers on his desk.

Holding a computer readout, Otto Albrecht walked out of the large data processing room at the Institute with a smile on his face. He was with an expert on biomechanics in running.

"Impressive," said Albrecht, pleased that the pieces of his Boston siege were falling into place.

"He has the lungs of a fish," said the man.

"His lactic acid content, it seems to look better than usual," Albrecht said.

"He ran five miles the other day, averaging four minutes thirty seconds per mile. His lactic buildup was nothing. Franz Overbeck has never been better."

"Now about the American and that little man from Japan—what is his name?"

"Sato," said the man. "Of course, from the available evidence on the American, Holt, we know that he was a very fine specimen."

"Not anymore," said Albrecht. "He will be merely going through the motions in Boston."

"He has never done that before."

"Well, he is not the same," said Otto.

"The Japanese is no worry. His record of 2:03 came on a very fast course."

"Like ice," Albrecht laughed. "I doubt if he has ever run up a hill in his life."

"There is one thing. The Japanese have a much lower body temperature than other people."

"So?"

"Just a fact," the man said.

"Keep me informed," Otto said, quickening his step and turning off the corridor.

He walked into another large room, filled with elaborate apparatus and white-smocked technicians with clipboards in their hands. He looked over at the treadmill. Franz was in his tenth mile, with the spirometer in his mouth, his bare chest fastened to the ECG hookup. Otto walked over to the treadmill and said to the technician, "That will be all." Then he walked with Franz to the massage room.

Albrecht watched as the masseur began to put the first rub on Franz's body, which was covered only by a towel. Finally, Albrecht waved the masseur out. "You can finish later." Franz sat up on the edge of the table, and Albrecht paced up and down in front of him, looking down at his squeaking shoes.

"You look fit," said Albrecht. "No problems."

"I would like to know about Boston soon," Franz said. Sweat dropped from his upper lip and chin.

"How do you know I'm interested in Boston?" Albrecht asked, glancing up.

"All the work we are doing. The tests. It's not usual unless there is a big race."

"Of course. You're an old hand. Why shouldn't you see that?"

"Am I going, sir?"

"Very anxious, Herr Overbeck. You never get anxious about a race."

"It is the perfect race for me now."

"For us," said Albrecht. He thought of Krueger's words, 'Nobody hunts alone, Otto.'

"For the country," Franz said. He reflected on Willy's phone call—'He's going to let you go to Boston'—and then said, "It is not necessary to go. It matters little to me. There are many races." He watched Albrecht walk back and forth.

"Yes, yes," Albrecht said. "But I did not say you were not going, did I?"

"I only do what you say, sir."

"You know Willy searched your rooms."

"He found nothing."

"I told him to do it," said Albrecht, searching his face with quick glances.

"You have to be informed."

Albrecht continued to pace, then said softly, "Why does a man run every morning to the same place and stare up at an elk?"

"Willy told you that?"

"Certainly. It is peculiar."

"A habit. What else could it be?"

Albrecht pulled out a pad, then looked at some scribbling. "I gave our psychologists this odd information," he lied. "Do you like animals?"

"I was just fascinated."

"So is the psychologist. He says that you were not looking at an elk. You were looking at freedom. That you do not feel free. Is that so?"

"That is above my head, sir."

"Such a man could do strange things. Especially in America."

"Again," said Franz, "I do not have to go."

Albrecht looked straight into Franz's eyes. His voice was still low. "I was thinking about Greta. What a beautiful woman. They talk about our East German women like they are animals. But not your Greta. She must be doing well with her beauty. An expensive whore by now, I should think. New York is filled with beautiful whores. Greta must be very rich. Not so?"

"Most likely," said Franz, keeping his eyes on Albrecht.

"Most likely what? That she is a . . . a filthy, syphilitic whore. Filled every week with the rotten sperm of a least two dozen men." Albrecht watched a drop of sweat run down Franz's nose, lingered with it as it hung on the tip. He was that close to him. Franz wanted to avert his eyes, yet he knew if he did he would drive his fist into Albrecht's nose.

"No doubt," said Franz.

The answer brought a curious tilt to Albrecht's head. Then he spun on his heel and walked off, saying, "You will hear from me soon, Herr Overbeck. Stay fit."

Franz lay back down on the table. The masseur entered and began his work.

"Go real deep," Franz told the masseur.

Little Smith was trying to sleep in the back of the car. "You think he has a license?"

"That's the least we can hope for," said Big, looking at his watch. "She'll be out soon. It's near eleven."

"He sounded like a doc on the phone," said Little, climbing into the front seat.

They sat there silently. You run out of talk when you have spent half your life together in a car, waiting, looking, for there is only so much you can get out of new diets, new restaurants or retirement plans. They watched the fine spray of rain turn the street into a soft, glistening surface, watched the forms of night hunters drift along the street, from an old bag lady to a young man who had made three trips up and down the street.

"There he goes again," said Big. "What's he looking for?"

"Take your pick. Maybe he's got amnesia and can't find where he lives."

"I'm here," said Big Smith, shaking his head. "I'm waiting. But I still can't believe it."

"Love ain't natural," said Little.

"Noses," said Big. "What the hell does a nose look like when it falls off!"

"You should've looked at the doc's pictures."

"I can't believe she'd take a chance on a doc from a newspaper ad."

"Here she comes!" said Little, pointing.

Greta moved rapidly up the street. She was wearing jeans tucked into high boots, a raincoat and a hat that looked as if it was out of the thirties.

"Keep your eye on the cowboy," said Big Smith. "He's getting close to her." He eased the car up the street. Greta was waiting at the curb for a taxi, and suddenly the cowboy was next to her. She gave him a hard look and walked fast down Third Avenue. The young man was getting ready to follow her when Big Smith wheeled the car up next to him and Little shouted, "Get the fuck outta here, sonny!"

"She's got a taxi," said Big Smith. The car wheels squealed, and they left the cowboy screaming on the corner.

"Listen to him yell," said Little. "If I was a cop, they'd have to pick up my piece the first night out."

They followed Greta's taxi down Second Avenue to the East Village. She got out in front of a weary old tenement with one of its fire escapes half hanging off. She entered the house, and the Smith Brothers hurried out of the car and

125

into the building. There were four flights of dimly lit stairs. They could hear them creaking under Greta's feet. They waited. "She's going to the top floor," whispered Little Smith as both of them stood rigidly at the bottom of the stairs. They heard a door open and voices. "Come on," said Big Smith.

Greta walked into the apartment. Her eyes moved around the front room. There were stuffed teddy bears whose button eyes had long ago been torn out by the cats who curled around her feet. There was a smell of dampness along with incense. Dust covered a long table littered with books, one leg of which was propped up by medical journals. Springs poked out of the couch, where the cats were fighting now. The man angled his head and looked into her face. He was slight, with the complexion of a spoiled orange. He was in his forties, had dark bags under his eyes and a bald pate that sat between two crops of rising, almost electrified hair. He did not introduce himself.

"Do not let my rooms disturb you," he said. "I do quality work. Did you bring the money?"

Greta handed him an envelope. He counted the money, the three thousand she had borrowed from a bank. He led her into the next room.

"Sit down there, please," he said. He pointed to an old barber's chair. Greta looked nervously around the room, then she focused on the tray of instruments.

"Now just lay back," said the man. "Relax. So we can get a look at what must be done." His fingers moved over her face. She noticed dirt under his nails.

"Beautiful bones," he said.

"Will it take long?" she asked, the skin on her face pale and taut.

"An hour or so." He rubbed his finger in the corner of

126

his eye. "A little nick here, a cut there. That's all. It will give your eyes a slanted effect."

"Will I look different?" she asked, worried that her face would still be recognized in East Germany.

"Some. But I think your nose should be broken for a complete change. You won't feel any pain. I'll give you a shot."

"I don't have any more money," said Greta.

"No extra charge. I figured it into the three thousand. People trying to duck the law always want their noses broken."

"Will it be a long time healing?"

"Four weeks or so. The cops'll never know you."

By now the Smith Brothers were on the top floor, where there were two apartments. They looked at both doors. "Which one?" asked Little. "Time's running out."

"I don't hear any voices," said Big, listening at one door.

"None over here, either," said Little.

"Let's try this one," said Big.

They tried the doorknob, turning it slowly. It wasn't locked. They moved the door open inch by inch. They heard the padding of tiny feet. Then, with a little push, they could see the whole room, and then only the huge face of a wolf, baring its yellow teeth, growling, its weight on its haunches and poised to leap. It did. The Smith Brothers jumped back, nearly falling over each other as they went for their guns. But the animal backed off as a command came from inside the room.

"A goddamn wolf!" said Little Smith, still holding his gun.

The Smith Brothers looked at the two figures on the

couch. The wolf sat under them stiffly. They were in hot pants that showed smooth, muscled legs. Their faces were heavily made up like those in a wax museum.

"Sorry, ladies," said Big Smith. "We made a mistake."

"You bet your ass you did," said one huskily.

They slackened their jaws. "Men," said Little Smith.

Big Smith flashed his wallet at the pair, putting his finger to his lips. He moved out of the room and over to the other door. The painted men, holding each other's hands, and the wolf stood in the doorway and watched as Big started to jimmy the lock.

"You couldn't open a can with a can opener," said one of the men.

"We making fun of you?" said Big, scowling.

"Get to work," said Little, his eyes still on the wolf.

Greta's body was floating in the barber's chair. She could only mumble now. The ceiling seemed a wave of liquid. Nooooo, she thought, struggling to get up. Numbness swept over her.

"Now, now," said the man, "you'll be just fine." He mopped the sweat from her forehead. "I know this procedure. I could do it blindfolded." He waited for her to go completely under. He heard the sudden yowl of a cat in pain. He started out to see what had happened, then saw that Greta was ready. He picked up a scalpel off the tray, looking at its glow in the sharp light. He straightened Greta's head, peered at her creamy skin and moved the scalpel toward the corner of her eye.

"Hold it!" yelled Big Smith as the two of them slammed into the room.

The man dropped the scalpel.

"You have to pass on this one, Doc," said Little.

Little gathered up Greta in his arms. "Call an ambulance," he told Big Smith.

"Only a standard injection," said the man. "Nothing heavy. I know my work."

"Did he nick her anywhere?" Big Smith asked.

"Not a mark," his partner said. "She's just out like a light."

"Get her money," Little said.

Big Smith called an ambulance, then dialed the nineteenth precinct. "Whitey, it's me," said Big Smith. "We got a doc here without an office."

The man sat down on the floor. Big Smith looked the place over while Little counted Greta's money. Big Smith was studying the tray of instruments. "What's this for?" he asked, holding up a small steel mallet.

"I break the nose," said the man. "Customary for jobs on felons. Why does the law want her?"

"She's a bad case of love," said Big.

"You mean the law doesn't want her? Her lover must be hard to please."

"Look at him," said Little. "Sitting there cold as an ice ball. You'd think he was at the top of his game."

"I was once," said the man, lifting his head arrogantly.

"He'll be out on the street in a few days," said Big. "Then another place, another town. Right, Doc?"

"I'll be out in a couple of hours," said the man. "And I won't go anywhere. I love New York."

He was still laughing when the cops came.

11

Roy woke to the faint cries of a coyote howling its pack home, the sputtering tail of the night wind and Buck's snoring. He raised himself on his elbows and looked over at the old man, his nose sticking out of Indian blankets, droning and scanning the area like radar. Roy climbed into his running pants, put on a Windbreaker and walked outside, looking up at the huge, glassy sky.

There were only two periods when you could run in Death Valley: in the morning before the sun came up and later in the evening when all the other creatures made their rounds under a cooling moon and sighing wind. Roy washed and toweled his face on the porch, then came back into the room. He slipped into his running shoes while looking at his mileage chart on a table next to a kerosene lamp.

"Nine hundred miles," Buck said, opening an eye. "Exactly."

"For six weeks," Roy said. "Close to two hundred a week. Haven't worked like that in a long time."

Buck pulled on his pants, and they took the Jeep out to the desert to the marked-off course that slipped between petrified rocks, along the crumbling skulls of long-dead animals, through the towering sand dunes whose color and whorl never seemed the same each morning; Roy had worked this course for twenty miles before sunup and nine more in the evening, six days a week for the last two weeks.

"Just go out a mile and back," Buck said. "We're going to work there today." He pointed in back of him to a dune 150 feet high, blue-white and still in the half-light.

"Not again, Buck," Roy said.

"We need it for the legs."

"We?" Roy said. "Me, you mean."

"You've been around the fights," Buck said, smiling. "You ever see a manager get hit?"

Roy jogged out over the course, and Buck walked over and stood at the bottom of the dune. He mumbled something, then began his climb slowly, his hands out like the two paws of a desperate animal clawing at the sand, his legs giving beneath him. "Sonuvabitch!" he kept yelling as he gained twenty feet and skidded back ten. Halfway up, he stopped and fought for breath, then resumed, thinking, All I'm doing is walking. That poor bastard's been running up here for weeks. He scratched his way up for another twenty minutes, and then he was at the top, puffing and mopping his brow as Roy jogged up to its base.

Buck looked down. The wind rippled across the sand. Roy backed off and hit the dune full speed, his feet digging into the sand, the knees pumping high. His thrust took him up a quarter of the way, but it soon faded. He could count only on his muscle and will against a repetitive drill that he had begun to hate. He kept falling, and Buck knelt at the top and stared wide-eyed at the broken motion, the flailing

131

arms below him. Roy looked as if he was going to stop.

"Don't you quit on me!" Buck screamed.

Roy was about three-quarters of the way up, and if he wasn't running he wasn't walking, either. He looked more like a man trying to run in deep water. The high-pitched voice of Buck cracked across the desert quiet.

"More! More! Ya hear me, Roy! Give me more!"

Roy pushed, coiled and uncoiled, and then his motion seemed to stop. He was standing straight up, a man trying to keep his balance on a high ledge.

"Quit! You're going to quit!" Buck was jumping up and down. Roy tottered, started doing a backstroke in the air. "Noooooo! Hold on, Roy!"

Roy regained his poise, bowed his neck and shoulders and dug his legs in like a big football tackle getting ready to bust into a blocking device. The sand kicked up in back of him. He spurted for the summit.

"Go! Go! Go!" Buck shouted.

With the last propulsion left in him, Roy threw himself at Buck's feet, his back heaving, his hair and gray sweat suit dripping wet.

"We made it," Buck said, looking down at him.

"*We* always do," Roy said. "I've been up this bastard sixty times since I've been here."

Roy gave Buck a slight push, sending him rolling down the dune, the sand flying about him, and then Roy began his own roll as daylight began to break over the blue desert.

Training—the steady, daily miles, the aloneness of the chase—is often layered in mystery in certain marathon quarters. But men and women get ready in every sport the same way. They sweat. They must throw themselves up

hard against the tedium of crushing routine. For all the eso-
terica of marathon training—bizarre diets, the intricate
methods of daily work with various stamps of approval—
Buck felt that there were no real secrets.

"An ocean of bull," Buck said, preparing spaghetti later
that night. He looked over at Roy, who seemed to be in a
daze on his cot. "Right, Roy? Grist for the obscurists. The
Americans love to pound everything into minute specializa-
tion."

World-class or first-timer, Buck thought, there was only
one way to get ready for a marathon: you logged the miles,
or you paid later. The top runners worked on speed and
distance, perfected the blend. They had a feel for it. They
knew. Buck stirred the spaghetti sauce and went on: "But
who knows about the mind, eh, Roy? It can snap a good
body in two during a race. Oh, the mind's a devil. For the
top guys. Even for the guy just trying to finish."

Buck lifted his eyes from the sauce toward Roy's bunk.
"You hear me? The mind . . ." He tasted the sauce.

Roy was sleeping.

The days passed, and Roy blasted grimly into each day's
work. He tore at the four hundred meter speed drills—
sometimes as many as twenty a day—like a man ripping off
the leg of a carcass. Buck would follow in the Jeep, one
eye on the course, the other on the stopwatch in his palm,
his mouth sometimes agape at Roy's assault on time.

At night, sitting on the porch and listening to the mourn-
ful creak of the old shacks, they exhausted topics of exchange, and then they grew quiet, because they did not
want to talk about the barrier or the Boston race, though
its nearness was starting to press down on them. Then Buck

made up his mind that if they didn't stop working the edges, somehow Roy might become spooked and start to act like a lot of top runners who ignored talk of a two-hour marathon as if it were an Egyptian curse concealed in some dark, clammy room.

Buck began in a positive way, ticking off Roy's physical assets for such a race. Lungs? Back in college Roy had had the highest oxygen uptake in world running: 89.5. His oxygen needs were very low. But most of all, there were the muscles in his legs. A muscle biopsy once showed this: he had slow-twitch muscles for endurance and the fast-twitch muscles of a sprinter. Plus, there was a third kind, a fiber that seemed to resist fatigue.

They knew the Japanese would be in Boston, and when Roy had called the Boston officials a few weeks before there was a rumor that the East German, Overbeck, might be there, too; Roy didn't believe it. Buck talked of the Japanese, saying: "They all have a low body temperature. Thirty-five centigrade. Lower than Caucasians. They don't like the cold. They don't like cold water. To drink or otherwise. You won't see a Jap touch a drop of water. They think it's a sign of weakness. He'll want a warm day."

"I need a cool, overcast day," Roy said.

"If it's sunny and warm," Buck said, "you won't even come near two hours."

They talked of time, the fierce, nerve-racking attack on the clock that had to pulsate like a firefly's glow. The two-hour pace called for four-minute thirty-second miles to Heartbreak Hill, ninety minutes to do twenty miles. He would lose time on that hill, but soon after he'd have to accelerate to a searing 4:30 pace and stay on it like Saint Elmo's fire over the last six miles.

"You'll be hurting now," Buck said.

"I can feel it already," Roy smiled.

"The pace softens you up for the killer—dehydration. You can't avoid it. First degree. Second degree. Third degree, and then they have to scrape you off the ground."

Roy thought of Oslo, felt the dread rising in him. Dehydration—close to third degree—had caused the horror of Oslo; how close, he wondered, had he come to death there? He knew the fear of the Oslo effects would be on his back over those last six miles. Buck had advised earlier how to deflect the fear. Late in the race, he should shift his focus away from time to the Japanese and the East German—if they were still with him. They would give him a hold on reality. They were less spectral than *time*.

Roy said, "The East German says it's a death race. You believe that, Buck?"

"Who knows?" Buck said, "You're fit. But that kind of pace . . . The dehydration. The body temperature up as high as a hundred and five. It's like a dangerous fever. The marathon is violence committed on the body. You know that."

"No flowers," Roy said. "Just have a drink on me." A terrible doubt seemed to wrap around him. "Why, Buck? Why am I doing this? Why can't I let it go, be normal? Am I hooked? Like a punched-up fighter?"

Buck didn't answer. He measured the question from all that he knew about Roy. The Ulysses impulse, thought Buck. The man who was driven to go farther and faster, who must see what's over the mountain, though there might be no practical value at all for humankind. The value was only in the true, instinctual deed, the basic reflection of man's search for himself. That was Roy. From their earliest days together, Buck knew that if Roy despised one thing it was being a person who floated through life and then left

135

it without ever having touched or felt or seen his own true center.

"There are two kinds of people, maybe," Buck said. "The useless who know it, and the useless who don't know it."

"And I don't know it?"

"No, you're a third kind," Buck said. "The Ulysses figure. You can't help yourself. You have to search, to risk. Like Hillary. Chichester. You don't want to know about limits. Think of that over those last miles up there, those last yards, when your body's screaming, and then slam into that *second wind*. The all-out push! Lift yourself up like a rocket from gravity!"

Roy was moved by the old man's sudden passion, his sparkling eyes. He listened for a moment to the wind sough and tinkle the window glass across the street, and said, "Buck, I hope you live forever. I wish I could do something for you."

"Just give me quality," Buck said, turning his head toward him. "There's not much around anymore."

12

Kanji exploded out of a series of long speed intervals in the first light of a damp, gray day, the kind of day when the trees seemed to come down the slopes and march into town behind the mist. He slowed down, moving past the stone lanterns outside of houses, then past the temples and pavilions of dark wooden interiors, finally ending up along the string of geisha restaurants sitting on the riverbank, their wind-bells tinkling sadly as if all the geisha inside were lying there with slender wrists trickling blood.

As he ran, Kanji threw up the image of himself as a runner. He saw clearly now that there was no relation between the pre-Rai runner and the Kanji who was much more than raw speed. He felt that he was now a runner of grace, with control and discipline. His stride was fluid and clean. His concentration was so intense that often he saw the miles having been run before he even slapped a foot down on the streets of Kyoto. He could barely hear his own breath.

By now, he was breathing the *ki-ai* way over three thousand times a day, and lately he had been slipping into a trance that was like a daydream, only lasting much longer, five minutes the first time, now well over a half hour. He was eager to be tested by Rai. The kitchen scene of Rai, himself and the red-hot poker was indelible in his mind. That night he went to Rai and said, "Test me again with the poker."

Rai did not say anything, and Kanji knew better than to press his request. But the next afternoon, Rai came to his room and said, "Come."

They walked for two miles beyond the monastery, and then Rai told him to sit down in front of a thick tree. Kanji watched him leave. He was going to be tested. The posture was easy for him now, and slowly, by breathing, he began to transmit all the energy of his being to the *tanden*, his lower belly.

Over an hour passed before Rai returned, a figure in a trailing orange robe topped by a somber hood, walking through the woods, carrying an ancient six-foot bow and a single arrow in his hand. The monk sat down in front of Kanji, twenty yards away. He withdrew a bamboo flute from his robe and began playing. They sat there for a good while before the music stopped, allowing the hush of the woods to return.

Then Rai stood up, his feet perfectly placed, his magnificent head and body turned sideways to Kanji, and positioned his long bow and drew his arrow into place. He brought it back down again, took out a blindfold and wrapped it around his eyes. Then he assumed his position with the bow again. For long minutes, the bow and arrow did not move. It was fixed there as if it were a still life of crafted wood and strained muscle. Then the arrow was gone, with a hissing sound of wood against air. It quivered four inches above Kanji's head.

Two days later Rai arranged for Kanji to go to Nara, one of the oldest cities in Japan and not far from Kyoto. Kanji was to stay there and return only when he wanted to. He would have to run earlier in the morning and later at night, and he would sleep in the forge of a Nara sword maker. He was going to watch the making of a samurai blade, once called the steel bible of Japan. The sword maker was one of the "human treasures" of the country. *Gassan* was his title, and only one other man was called that in the nation. Each morning before starting work, the *gassan* went to a Shinto shrine and prayed.

After his early morning workout, Kanji took up his place in the forge, a kneeling place in a corner next to a tatami mat on which he slept. The *gassan* never seemed aware of his presence. The artisan wore a loose white robe and the classic *eboshi*, a black, lacquered hat. There was no talk while he and his apprentices, one of whom would inherit his title, worked, their eyes riveted to the strip of red steel on the anvil, their hands guiding it by tongs in and out of a hearth that was up to 2,000 degrees Fahrenheit.

The glowing color of the strip told them when to withdraw it from the hearth, and then they would lay it on the anvil, the signal for his apprentices to begin pounding it with odd-size hammers, filling the forge with long chords of hypnotic, dissonant musical tones. Then the strip of steel was folded back upon itself, the thousands of fused layers bringing to the blade immense strength and flexibility; no one knew exactly how many layers—thirty thousand, some said—were in a samurai blade, for it was a secret known only to the *gassan*.

Continuing his breathing, Kanji watched every move amid the heat and dancing sparks, and he could see how the craftsmen seemed to become the sword, the very object itself. Like a maple leaf breaching a bamboo fence. From his first day there he, too, had been sending his body and mind through the process, feeling the hearth, the hammers and the immersion of himself into cold, tempering water. He had lost all sense of time. And then one day the *gassan* walked outside and held his sword up to the sun, catching the sun in a certain way and studying the beams, because he knew he would never see the same ones again. Kanji looked up into the light and saw only himself.

Back with Rai, and only four days before he had to go to Boston, Kanji said, "Give me the poker. I will grasp it now."

"What did you see in Nara? asked Rai.

"I am a sword," Kanji said, thinking of how he now ran the miles like a blade whistling through wind.

"Let us look at your sword," Rai said.

"The poker?" Kanji asked.

"A room," the priest said, knowing that Kanji, for all his enormous progress, would not be equal to the test by fire.

Rai picked up the samurai blade of Takamori, the heirloom handed down for generations by his grandfather, the steel that had once dripped blood and pure motive. He handed it to Kanji, and they walked out across the grounds to a small building. Inside, there was a small room the size of a large closet, containing only a tiny rectangle of a viewing window big enough for a pair of eyes. Rai put Kanji in the room, turned the light on and said before leaving, "Withdraw the sword and hold it straight up in front of your eyes."

After two hours, Rai returned and put his eyes up against the window outside. He studied the posture of Kanji, the way he was breathing, and then the attitude of the blade he was holding; clasped by both of Kanji's hands at the handle, the sword was still upright and rigid. Rai then walked around to the side of the closetlike room, looked at a lever on the wall and pulled it down, releasing a slat inside the room.

Rai moved his eyes to the window again. This time Kanji was not alone. By pulling the lever, Rai had sent a thousand fat mosquitoes into the hot, bright room. Rai had gotten them from the research lab at Kyoto University. Centuries before—though not often anymore—mosquitoes had been used to test the state of trance in monks or the desired plateau of samurai warriors "to live as if they were already dead."

Rai watched. The mosquitoes swarmed in a cloud under the low ceiling, then hundreds of them dotted it, and the rest crusted the single light bulb, dimming the room. Rai kept his eyes on Kanji, his hands, his face, his almond eyes. Kanji didn't stir. His eyes were empty. There was nothing on his face, not even a flutter along the jawline. Rai could see only the force rushing to the power center on Kanji's lower body.

Then, like a piece of lint falling through the air, a mosquito dropped down on Kanji's shaved head. It sat there and then began to ease over the skull and down the center of the forehead. Rai could see Kanji's hands tighten their grip, his eyes burning into the blade of his grandfather's sword. The sweat poured off his face, and now there were four, ten, a dozen, scores of mosquitoes on Kanji's face, stuck to the sweat on his lips, his eyelids, his ears.

Rai watched for two more long minutes and then said to himself, "Now."

Kanji did not move, and the sword in his hands wavered slightly. His face was still covered with mosquitoes.

"Now," said Rai, "now."

Then, at last, he saw Kanji build the final, long intake of breath, and then he loosed the *ki-ai* from its power center, sent it flowing up into an otherworldly sound: aaaaaa-aaaaaaah hhhhhhhhhhh gggggggggggggggggeeeeeeeeeeeee-hhhhhhhhhhhhhhhhmmmmmmmmmph!!! The mosquitoes moved back to the light bulb and ceiling.

Rai opened the door and lifted Kanji to his feet. He toweled Kanji's face with the sleeve of his robe. He then examined his face closely while running his long finger over his skin.

There was not a mark, a bump or a red bite on Kanji's face.

"You bring me honor," Rai said.

Two days later, Kanji was ready to leave Rai and Mount Hiei. The priest came into the room and sat next to him on the tatami mat.

"I don't know what to say," Kanji said, once more in his Western clothes of sport jacket and slacks, his bald head freshly shaved. "You have done so much for me."

"There is nothing to say," Rai said. "You have spoken with your progress."

"Come with me," Kanji said. "Come to Boston."

"No, but I will be with you."

"I will never be the same again."

"It is up to you," the priest said. "I will tell you a small tale. I was a very young man and had gone to the mountains to live and study with a man of rare power. For years, scholars as well as skeptics from all over the world had come to see him. Some had seen his power with their own eyes. And still did not believe. Others called him supernatural. He made no claims. He knew that the power in him was the power that was in all men, if they would search for it and nourish it."

Kanji thought, These are more words than he has spoken during my whole time here. Rai went on: "One day he became very sick. I could feel the cancer eating at his body. A former student and doctor was called to visit him. The man told him that he had two months to live. The holy man listened and then went off into the woods. When he returned, he appeared like a new man. The doctor was called again. Examining him, he was amazed. This could not be true. The cancer was gone. The holy man had driven it from his body."

"How?" Kanji asked.

"Through *ki-ai* and trance," Rai said. He continued: The people in the villages, the woodsmen could not believe their eyes. The holy man was reborn. Months, a year, ten years passed. And each day the holy man would take a long walk at daylight in the woods. And always, because he was barefoot, the woodsmen swept his path clean of thorns. Then one day, while he was walking, he stepped on a thorn. He flew into a horrible rage, and it washed over him like an angry wave. He screamed to the sky at those who had not cleared the path. Three weeks later, he was dead of the same cancer."

They sat there, and Kanji finally said, "A tiny thorn."

"Destroyed the force within him," Rai said. They walked to the temple gate. Kanji looked down the hill and saw that Ichy was waiting for him by the car. Rai handed Kanji a piece of paper, which he opened and read.

"A black ball ran rolling into the pitch-black night," Kanji said. "A koan?"

"Keep it in your mind," said Rai. "And I will be next to you."

Rai turned and strode toward the temple.

13

Lunch was over at Kurt Mueller's house, and now he and Franz strolled through one of Leipzig's little parks while Kurt's children skipped along in front of them. It was Sunday afternoon, bright, with promise all around them; flowers were budding and the trees were becoming fat and green again. In another time in the same park, they might have been two business associates out for a Sunday promenade with their children, two prosperous Eastern Europeans wearing wing collars and serious vests holding pocket watches, trying to listen to themselves over the music of the park band.

"My father," said Kurt, "used to come here as a young man before the war. This was the place to be on Sundays. For young couples, for families to show off their children. For men to exchange information."

"Must have been simple back then," said Franz.

"Living," said Kurt. "I don't think it's ever been simple."

"The park doesn't seem to fit here now," Franz said,

looking up at the high blocks of sterile apartment units that encircled them.

The three children, two boys and a girl, shouted at Kurt, asking if they could get on the swings. Kurt waved his permission, and then he and Franz sat down on a bench. They sat quietly for a while, listening to the shrieks of the children, whose golden hair flashed in the sunlight.

Then Mueller said, "There are rumors."

"Oh?" said Franz. "What kind of rumors?"

"That you are going to Boston."

"Perhaps. But you will be going, too."

"I hope not," Kurt said, his eyes following the arcs of the swings.

"Why?" Franz asked. "You have always been with me."

"I just have a feeling. That it is not going to be routine there."

Franz owed Kurt an honest answer. He wanted to tell him about his feelings for Greta. But Kurt was still a security man. It was his life: like the three children on the swings, his wife at home, the splendid apartment in one of the better buildings. He would have to tell the head of the force, who would tell Albrecht. Boston would be finished.

"Something that I should know?" Kurt asked. "About you and Greta? You see, I believe that you are not a rash man."

"I did make a request for Boston," Franz said.

"I know. Then you probably regretted it."

"I want to go."

"But why?"

"Because I'm a runner and that's where I should be."

"But why this Boston Marathon? Why not last year's, or the one before that?"

"Like you, I have a feeling. Only I want to be there."

"Tell me the truth," Kurt said. "Could you be so foolish as to give up your status, your recognition here for your wife?"

Franz did not falter. "Never." The answer sounded firm, unassailable, far from the ambiguity of his own mind.

"Good," Kurt said. "But I will still request not to go."

"It is up to you, Kurt," Franz said, hoping that his friend would not be sent to Boston; Kurt would only be more pressure on him.

The children came running to Franz, who caught the little girl in his arms.

"Give us a push, Uncle Franz!" she shouted. "So high." She pointed upward. "High up to the sky."

Monday morning, three weeks from Boston, was a busy day for Otto Albrecht. He first had to meet some journalists from England, then there was a meeting with psychologists in the afternoon. He was running out of time on his decision about Overbeck and Boston; he'd have to make it within three days.

Like so much else, Otto did not like journalists, especially those from abroad. They were prying. They were clever, with their unruly questions that slowly tightened on an answer they wanted. And they were all potential spies, people who wanted secrets about East German athletics.

Albrecht led the tour over the Institute's grounds, trying to avoid strident comments about the West, keeping his answers dry and to the point.

Pushing past Otto's matter-of-fact style, one journalist asked, "Is it true that all of your athletes are under oath not to divulge secrets about your program?"

"Not so," Albrecht said sharply. "When beaten, some

people always look for an excuse for losing. We have no secrets. We only work harder." They passed a large group of
young boys, aged twelve to fifteen, working out on a track.

Albrecht pointed. "They are our only secrets. They belong to one of our best sports schools. Their studies are
built around their athletic programs. They have the best
teachers, the best medical attention."

"How do you pick and choose?"

"We have sports managers who watch them. They visit
homes and convince parents of the honor of going to one of
these schools." He did not say that the parents were often
relocated near the schools, given better jobs and quarters.

"And if they do not progress?" asked another reporter.

"Our elite men must meet certain standards to stay in the
program. So must the young ones. A boy who runs fifteen
hundred meters in four minutes fifteen seconds must run
that same distance the next year by nine seconds less. If he
does not move forward, he goes back to a standard school."

"The budget must be tremendous for all this?"

"Grants produce money for the clubs and schools. The
Ministry of Education funds the Institute, which trains
coaches and sports doctors. Businessmen must give up eight
percent of their profits to various programs. Workers give
one day's wages each year."

"And the top runners? What do they get out of it?"

"Much," said Otto. He wanted to compare them to
American athletes who had to accept money under the
table in order to train and survive; he refrained. "Official
honors. Pensions years later. Room and board in a dormi-
tory. We all took a cruise after Montreal. To Cuba."

"I'd rather go to Rumania," mumbled some one in the
crowd.

Otto did not hear him; he went on. "Good careers later.

Education. Clothes. Tickets to events. Much prestige. Television must give twenty-five percent of its programs to sports."

"Then someone like Franz Overbeck is a national hero?"

"Franz Overbeck is, of course, well-known," said Otto. "He is looked up to by the young. But gentlemen, you are missing the point. The real hero is our program. We must not forget."

"What is the attitude toward his wife, Greta?"

"Irrelevant question," said Otto, looking back to try to pick out the voice.

They walked to the Institute, and Otto moved them hurriedly from one room to the next. The journalists scribbled in their note pads.

"Just like the American space program of the sixties," said one of them.

Otto liked that comparison. He showed them an immense computer. "The making of the super East German athlete is a national goal."

"What comes out of here?" came a question.

Albrecht patted the computer. "The future champions," he said. "Tests that are being done on young boys. A screening process."

He resisted the temptation to go further. To tell them of the bone X rays that could predict final body size; body fat that could be checked by skin-fold measures; analysis of the way an athlete runs, indicating aptitude for a certain event; pulse-rate data showing one's cardiovascular efficiency; endurance experiments; the measuring of muscle strength; tests for the capillaries. And there were more tests: intelligence, psychological, all of them designed to fit traits and style to events from the marathon to the sprint.

"It doesn't seem like sport," a journalist said.

Otto managed a grin. "How do you define sport? Is it sporting to let an athlete run a difficult race when his hemoglobin level is low? He could be ruined for six months. Should a man train over a hundred miles a week without first giving him an electrocardiogram? Any other way is the sport of fools."

"How does Overbeck measure up in the computer on a scale of one to ten?"

"I do not understand this 'one to ten,' " Otto said. "But he measures very, very high."

"No nagging injuries?"

"Perfect condition."

"How would you compare him to Roy Holt?"

Otto hesitated, then said, "The American is a fine runner. It would be unfair to compare him to Franz Overbeck. Unfair to the American."

"What about the Japanese and his record at Hiroshima not long ago?"

"Gentlemen," said Albrecht, trying to smile, "we have stopped being serious, haven't we? I must bid you a good day. Lunch is waiting for you in the Institute's cafeteria."

Albrecht studied the men around his desk, all of whom he knew and trusted, though more as scientists than as men; he had little faith in any man. He looked upon these men as highly productive, exquisite components in his monolith of brains. If he often derided the doe-eyed seers in America who wanted to make running the equivalent of religious dogma, who saw it as an evolutionary step in the development of man, he dared not underestimate psychology and its value to competitive running.

For all their fuzzy jargon, these were the men who

150

sprang the trapdoors of his athletes' minds, gave him a look into the one factor that defied his black-and-white code. They had advised him to use Willy Schmidt; they had spotted more than one troubled athlete for him. Otto listened to them. He needed them—now more than ever.

"We have here," Albrecht said, "what we can safely say is perfection." He opened Franz Overbeck's folder. "For the year 1983." He smiled blandly.

His eyes moved across the faces of the head psychologist and his assistants; under their guidance, there was a whole corps of eager and brilliant graduate students.

"Now, of course, you know why you are here," Albrecht said. "Only you can tell me how perfect he really is."

The head man began to speak, and Otto raised his hand. "Let me say first that I am considering certain things. Remember, this is a unique situation. Dangerously unique. I must know absolutely whether he can be trusted in Boston. First . . . I am considering a sodium pentothal test. Your comments, please."

"Very delicate," said the head man.

"I agree entirely," said an assistant.

"How so?" asked Albrecht, taken aback.

"Overbeck is not stupid," said the head man. "He will realize what was done. Right now, he is a model of body and mind. If the drug provides a negative result to our queries, shows that he has no intention to defect, it could damage him. Only an idiot would not feel some lack of trust after such a test. He feels now that we are his maker, his family. Having worked with him for years, I submit that he would be severely bothered by the distrust. In his case, I call it destructive."

"Nothing bothers him," said Otto.

"This would," said the head man.

"Moving on," said Otto, "let's talk then about a polygraph."

"Highly erratic," said the head man. "And self-defeating in our situation. Suppose there is a hint of emotion. Just a little. I believe it would be quite unnatural for him not to show some on the graph. Then what do you do? Keep him home because of a small spark caught by a machine that still is scientifically inaccurate? Give any number of divorced men such a test, even those violently hating their ex-wives, and you might find a speck of positive emotion. But does that mean they would go back to them? Hardly."

"Then what do you advise?" asked Albrecht, annoyed at their sniping comments.

"Leave him alone," the head man said. "Franz is an indifferent young man. His potential for other than surface feeling is quite low."

"He married, didn't he?" asked Otto. "That, I understand, requires passion."

"You must be reading too many romances," said the head man, grinning. "Marriage, believe me, is often an act of complete indifference to oneself."

"Thank you," Albrecht said. "I will weigh your advice."

"Do not tamper with him, Otto," the head man said.

Albrecht watched them leave. He thought of a jury that had condemned him to more anxiety, and he wondered: Why do they always travel in packs?

Monday night Albrecht made a phone call, then walked over to Emile Zweig's office. Zweig was the head of East German athletic security. Otto waited for him outside, feeling no twinge at all over what he was thinking. Zweig came

out, and they strolled through the evening shadows over
the grounds of the Institute. They were as friendly as either
of them could decently afford, considering the subtle inter-
necine warfare that was always being conducted within the
nervous belly of the Institute. Their wives were friends,
and the couples dined together once a month; Albrecht had
once gone to great lengths to keep Zweig's two sons in one
of the sports schools.

Zweig was a jovial, vulpine figure, a veteran of the Rus-
sian front in World War II. It was said that he owed his
present post to the Russians; he had many friends in Moscow. He had been a defector as well as a traitor during the
war, carrying with him a large bulk of intelligence toward
the end of the ragged campaign in eastern Germany; Zweig
was not one to go anywhere empty-handed.

Though Zweig's face was always crinkled in a smile and
his short frame long gone to suet, few dared to mistake his
happy exterior for a pulpy mind. He might look like he belonged on an Oktoberfest postcard, but he was a devious,
ruthless man, doctrinaire and implacable.

"So you have found a solution to your problem, Otto?"
Zweig asked.

"I think so," Albrecht said.

"Is that so? Well done, Otto."

"It is you."

Zweig stopped and laughed. "That is funny. I thought
you wanted to see me to invite me to dinner. But it isn't
that time of the month, is it?"

"You knew why."

"Surely. I knew it would come down to me. Everything
always does."

"I must be sure nothing will happen. That he cannot
defect."

"It is odd. I have never known you to be a gambler, Otto. Even when we have dinner out. The same restaurant all these years. You always order the same thing." He laughed again, holding his sides.

"I don't like surprises."

"You are telling me?"

"If anything went wrong in Boston, it would be terrible for the Republic and the Institute."

"You forgot yourself, Otto. I would not want to be in your shoes."

"I am aware."

"You would be a career vegetable. Maybe even charges that could keep you in prison for a long time. Fake ones, of course." His face was a shining grin, then he said seriously, "So why?"

"It is the right time," Albrecht said. "We didn't meet the Americans in the Olympics. We lose when they are not involved. We stand to gain heavily in prestige. America is like a mirror for us. Two images. Our way, and their way. Franz is right. The event is a big opportunity for us."

"Again, you forget. It is the right time for you."

"A triumph of courage and decision-making."

"It will rocket your career."

"The Russians would notice?"

"Most certainly. They are still angry at the American boycott of the Olympics in Moscow. You would give them something to chew on."

"I thought as much."

"More than that." Zweig drew the picture. "The GDR is Russia's favorite. The rest of the satellites have gone insane. Workers' strikes in Poland. They killed each other for blue jeans in Czechoslovakia. Yugoslavia sleeps with one foot in the White House. Disorder, uncertainty everywhere. But here . . . here the line was held."

"So . . . you see my point?" Albrecht asked, feeling more confident.

"Yes, and I also see the other end. It makes me quake."

"He will not defect."

"You only think. You do not know. The Rhine River runs between the two. You are talking about a man and a wife. A beautiful, strong woman. A separation of two years. One moment in a room. Alone. Can you feel it? Good-bye your Overbeck. And you, too, Otto."

"There is a remedy," said Albrecht, stopping under an elm tree. The darkness was falling quickly. Zweig lit his pipe.

"I want him killed if he defects," said Albrecht.

Blowing out his match, Zweig said, "And who gives you the sanction for this? Certainly not Krueger. Or the others."

"It is mine," said Albrecht. "Krueger told me to do what I must." He felt for the first time like a man who could see finally how far he was crawling above his ambition.

"And you are, dear Otto, you are. But I fail to see what I can get out of this."

"I will take you with me."

"To where? How far can I advance? I am old. Is this all you offer?"

"Your sons will be marrying soon. They will have children. You must plan the future for them and your grandchildren."

They walked a while without words until Zweig came to his car, then he said, "There is a way. Let me think about it."

MILES TO GO

* * *

Short of killing, stopping a defection was quite difficult; Zweig knew this. The other side needed only seconds, a minute to make the transition work, while those who guarded had to be always ready, listening for the creaking door, watching for the signs that the moment was near. It was guesswork—expensive, relentless and often absurdly speculative.

The East Germans had not lost an athlete since Greta Overbeck, nor had anyone gone over before her. Security had been tightened with Greta's jump. But Zweig knew that the absence of traffic was not mainly because of his vigilance. The desire, the motivation simply had not been there for the athletes, most of whom cared little about other environments.

Zweig had a hundred men in his department. He moved his finger down the roster, the details of their careers and skills jumping into his mind with each move of his chubby thumb. Some were political appointees, others did not have the brains of a good Doberman and were fit only for dropping messages or running errands. He then picked a pilot for a helicopter. Next he chose a quite expendable spotter, then took a bit more time in selecting a technician, the man for the trigger. Rapidly, he checked off five more names to be used as a surveillance team. Now he had to find a man to direct the operation. That was easy. The man was smart, dedicated and had been the most reliable in his department. He put a check by the name of Kurt Mueller.

Four nights later, while walking behind their wives to a restaurant, Zweig said, "I have a plan. But first I will tell you what I want, Otto."

"Anything," Albrecht said.

"I am old, Otto. I will have to bow out shortly. By that

time, if all goes well, you will have considerable power. What I want is this. A fine career for them. Assure me that eventually they will achieve the power of my department."

"Is that all?"

"Only one thing more. Make sure you look out for me when no one else cares."

"You can count on my memory."

"Good!" Zweig chirped. "Consider him dead."

"It won't come to that. What is your plan?"

"Expensive. Nine men in all. They'll use the cover of coaches and trainers."

"Is that enough?" Otto felt panic, now that Zweig had agreed.

"One cautious man should recognize another," Zweig said.

"Overbeck must not be alone."

"Three men will be with him at all times when he trains or relaxes."

"How about when he sleeps?"

"My control, the head of the operation, will sleep in the same room with him."

"It looks solid."

"Ahhhh, but you forgot the race. The one time he will be alone. He cannot be tracked by car. If he goes, I believe he will defect during the race. Otherwise, he will not have a chance."

A nerve jumped around Albrecht's eye; he had not thought of the race. "So, we are still vulnerable."

"Do you want to back off?"

"No, I just want to be certain that . . ."

"Rest easy, Otto. The plan will work."

"How? Who is your control?"

"How, I will not say. The control is Kurt Mueller."

"He is close to Franz. Can you trust him?"
"As much as you trust Overbeck."
"Overbeck will not defect. This is just precaution."
"Then there you are. Make your announcement."
"Tomorrow," Albrecht said.
"Are you relieved?" Zweig said.
"Slightly."
"The life of the gambler," Zweig said, laughing.

14

With a newspaper in his hand, Heinrich stood in the pool of shadow in the rear of the Church of Saint Thomas. It was noon, two and a half weeks before Boston, and he waited for his nephew. Learning of Franz's attempt to go to Boston weeks earlier, Heinrich had sent him an anonymous note, asking him if he was planning a trip, and if he was and was given clearance Franz should go the day after the news was public, precisely at noon, and sit in the last pew of the famous church.

Heinrich tried to relax by listening carefully to the rehearsal of the boys' choir, their voices and the booming organ making the dust particles bounce in the strips of light that fell on wine-dark, wooden pews. After ten more minutes, Franz rushed in and sat down in the last pew to the right. Heinrich watched, keeping his eyes on the back of Franz and the faces entering the church, mostly old and solemn women wearing black veils.

Heinrich walked over and stood in back of Franz, saying in a half-whisper: "You're five minutes late."

"I didn't want to be followed," Franz said, starting to turn.

"Don't turn," Heinrich said, a little louder.

Franz's eyes were startled by a sudden recognition. "Heinrich, it's you? I can't believe it."

"You asked me," Heinrich said, "if I'd ever help you take a trip."

"And you helped Greta?" Franz asked. "You were the one?"

"I had to," Heinrich said. "She was near a breakdown. She couldn't take the life here anymore."

"Had I known then," Franz said, "I would have strangled you."

Heinrich asked him for his itinerary. Franz told him that they were going straight to Boston, without the usual shopping detour to New York. The group would include two doctors, two trainers and nine security people. He didn't know yet who would be in control of the operation.

"Who would have thought Otto would take a chance like this," Heinrich said. "He must be sure of you."

"He doesn't know me," Franz said, annoyed.

"We shall see."

The choir and organ stopped. They could hear the choirmaster's voice up in the loft. Franz asked, "When will I see her?"

"Out of the question," Heinrich said.

"I want to be with her."

"Yes. If you defect. The Americans can't be bothered otherwise."

"How?"

Heinrich dropped a piece of paper to Franz's side, saying,

"Don't open it now. It is a map of the Boston course. You will see an X marked at a certain point. At Coolidge Corner. Twenty-two miles into the race."

"What should I do?" Franz asked.

"They will be watching you most of the race. By then, at the X, they will feel confident that nothing is going to happen. Turn off at the X. A car will be waiting. And so will Greta."

"So simple?"

"That depends on you. You must decide how you want to live the rest of your life. There won't be another chance. Albrecht and the Institute, or Greta."

"I hate Albrecht," Franz said, thinking back to how he had driven Willy to his death, of the filth that had run from his mouth about Greta. "What will you do, Uncle?"

Heinrich tossed the newspaper next to Franz. He heard the rap of the choirmaster's stick up in the loft. He wanted to place his hand on Franz's shoulder but pulled it back and started to walk toward the cathedral entrance.

"Uncle?" Franz asked.

Outside, Heinrich stood in the sun on the steps, listening for a moment to the choir and the celestial mathematics of Bach. He would try to go back to Bavaria where he had always belonged. He had raised his dead brother's son, had given Franz the only gift he had left—a chance at freedom. He drew a deep breath, brushed a drop of water from his rheumy eye and walked away, hoping that Franz was bigger than the Institute's years of design—that he had the courage of Greta.

Kurt Mueller never got a chance to submit his request not to go to Boston. He waited in Emile Zweig's office, sensing that he was about to hear something connected to Franz's trip. He was angry with himself. The trick in promotion or success was not to maneuver yourself or be maneuvered into a position where you could be caught in the hard algebra of goal, necessity and solution; a situation that could end your career.

Rosy-cheeked and with a twinkle in his eye, Zweig came out and walked Kurt into his office. He chattered on about how old he was feeling these days, how he would be retiring soon, then turned the talk to Mueller.

"I look at my roster," Zweig said, "and I keep saying to myself: Emile, who could take over my post? The answer always seems to end up with your name. And a few others, of course."

"Field men never rise that high," Kurt said.

"Yes, but you are not an ordinary field man," Zweig said. "Look at your record. You've been to the East Berlin intelligence school. You've had another six months in Moscow. People think highly of you, Kurt. You know how to act. You can handle men."

"I appreciate your good opinion," Kurt said.

"You have earned it." He changed the subject. "Your family? All is well? The children must be getting big. We must think of finding you a larger place. A big house, perhaps."

Kurt shifted in his chair and said, "We are happy."

"Good!" Zweig said. "I like contented men." Zweig clasped his hands behind his head and leaned back in his chair. "Now, Kurt, we have what could be a serious problem. You have been chosen to be the solution."

"Is it Franz Overbeck's trip?" Kurt asked, holding his breath.

"There you go," Zweig said, chuckling. "You are indeed always on your toes, Kurt."

"He is close to me and the family."

Zweig slammed in quickly. "Will he try to defect in Boston!"

Kurt stumbled, then said, "I don't think so."

"You don't think so," Zweig said. "But you don't know."

"One never knows completely what's on another man's mind."

"That, of course, is why you are here."

"You want me in Boston with him?" Kurt knew he couldn't decline; Zweig would break him down to a grubby surveillance man if he did.

"You will be with him," said Zweig. "You will head an eight-man team that will guard him around the clock."

"He's never any trouble."

"And if he is, there is a solution."

"What is it?"

"You see, if he defects, I believe he will go during the race. He is to be trailed throughout the race in a helicopter. Rent one there. I have already chosen the pilot and the spotter. And the man with the trigger."

"What trigger?" Kurt moved to the edge of his seat. "What . . ."

"Franz Overbeck will be killed if he goes over to them."

"This . . . I mean this is really guessing."

"That is all we have, Herr Mueller," said Zweig, his voice sober. "Overbeck as a defector would send a shock wave through East Germany, do you understand? It cannot happen."

"But—"

"Let me finish! There will be no bullets. Our man will use curare."

"Curare?" asked Kurt, as if talking to himself.

"He has worked with it before. You, Herr Mueller, will be on the ground. With a remote device. It's being prepared now. The spotter will tell you when Overbeck has been hit. Then you press the button and blow the helicopter up. There will be no trace of our hand in it anywhere. He will have been killed by a maniac U.S. patriot. They are always killing each other over there. It will be a very hot situation for them. I doubt if they will pursue it strongly. Unless we press. And we won't. Only superficially."

"I've never killed a man before."

"The curare will do that. As for the others, they are expendable."

"Franz is not expendable! He is the most honored athlete in our country!"

Zweig noticed the emotion in his voice. "The lesser of two considerations. The country or him. There can be no failure."

"I might as well be killing him," Kurt said.

"I'm sure I can count on you. It will be a big thing for your career."

"I have no choice," Kurt said, reflecting over the position that he could not struggle out of.

"You do not look like a contented man anymore, my dear Kurt."

"It's a strange feeling."

"Of course."

Zweig got up and walked him to the door, a fatherly arm crooked in Kurt's. Then, before saying good-bye, he leaned over and said firmly in a gravel voice, "For us. For your family. If Franz Overbeck defects, kill him!"

The Smith Brothers were in a taxi on their way into Boston from Logan Airport. They had told Greta about her husband's trip to America. She had flung herself into their arms, crying, and after she settled down her mind began to prepare the logistics for their meeting.

"No dice," Big Smith said.

"You get near him," Little said, "and they'll have him on the next plane back home."

Now the taxi pulled up to a small two-story row house near Harvard. There was a man peering out the front window, and before the Smith Brothers could knock, he was at the door.

"Come in," Soldier Burns said.

Well into his sixties, Soldier was a little too big to have been a jockey, and far too small to have been the retired bouncer suggested by his gnarled knuckles and sorely used face, on which the most serious impressions had been beat during his days as a Dublin street urchin and by a shovel on a tramp steamer when he had worked his way to Boston. He wore a cap and a scarf and, pouring tea for himself, seemed now a model of old age, of restraint and peace and thoughtfulness. And so he was, until any conversation began about the Boston Marathon. Then he would become alert or flinty, depending on what was being said and who was saying it; he allowed only one critic of the race—himself.

The Smiths had the book on him. Soldier was not the head of the Boston race, though he was the quiet character and spirit behind it. He had been linked with the race for over forty years. The press loved him. He was a landmark to the fans. And the new runners, who had punished themselves for months to get to Boston, hardly knew of him. The women runners never used to like him. He was for years an obstacle to their desire to run at Boston; when they finally beat his opposition, he was a gracious loser.

There was not much he could do about women anymore. There wasn't much he could do about anything: the mass of runners who threatened to make *his* race unmanageable; the few "showboating" runners who ran in absurd head-dresses and garish T-shirts, who mocked the dignity of *his* race; the wild cyclists who pirouetted among the runners and the discoing roller skaters on the course; and most despicable of all, the "crashers" who ran in the race without being officially entered.

"A drink?" Soldier asked.

"If you're having some?" Big said, settling into a deep chair and looking at all the running pictures on the wall.

"Don't touch it anymore," said Soldier. He poured some Scotch into their glasses.

"Thanks for your time," Little said.

"You have quite a race this year," Big said.

"Oh, it's going to be a beauty," said Soldier. "Nothing like it in a long time."

"Who do you like?"

"I know little about the Japanese. My friends in Japan tell me he has speed to burn. The East German? Never thought he would be here. He is strong, will be trained to the quick. But have you ever seen Roy Holt? A bloody wildcat, he is. If he's sound."

"We're here to talk to you about the East German," said Big Smith.

Soldier shot a glance at them, alert to the words that seemed to ring of intrusion on the sanctity and protocol of *his* race. "You got a mind to fool with my race, do you?"

"We have to give him a chance to defect," said Little.

Soldier glowered. "You're going to ruin my race, you are. I won't stand for it. Try it, and I'll have you in newspapers from Boston to Hong Kong."

"Now, hold it, " Big Smith said. "We only want your cooperation."

"You're not going to hurt the race?" Soldier asked.

"Certainly not," Big said. He could not tell him about their plan to have Overbeck turn off at Coolidge Corner; it would be enough to drive old Soldier into an apoplectic rage.

"Why come to me?"

"Because," Little said, "you run this race."

"Jock Semple runs this race," Soldier said, sipping his tea and smiling. "Haven't you heard that?"

"You both built it up to what it is," Big said. "You're his right hand."

The comment drew some fire. "I'm nobody's right hand," Soldier said, before lowering his voice. "Besides, I want no credit."

"You've fought long to keep this race a national classic," Big said.

"Don't butter me up," Soldier said. "It's bloody chaos. My race is already a mob scene out of D.W. Griffith."

"Just give us a picture of the race," Little said.

"From front to end," Big said. "Who is where . . . and doing what. That sort of thing."

"Will you help us?" Little asked.

Soldier gave them each a suspicious look and said, "Go on. I'll listen."

167

15

An April dawn broke over Boston.

Kanji Sato knelt before a miniature Shinto altar in his hotel room while the mammoth sumo wrestler, Ichy, slept, his Vesuvius belly rising and falling under the blankets.

Franz Overbeck was still sleeping in the bed next to the awakening Kurt Mueller.

Alone, Roy Holt lay in a dark room and stared at the window curtains.

Hours were left now before the eighty-sixth Boston Marathon, its unbroken continuity going back to 1897, the historical gasp of the Gilded Age, the era of Mark Twain, gaslights and robber barons. Gentleman Jim Corbett was the heavyweight champion of the world. Henry Ford's Model T was still eleven years away, and Thomas Edison was making the first moving pictures.

Now, with the jet plane as commonplace as the clang of the old streetcar, the moon no more just a lovers' beacon, the city of Boston got ready for another marathon, a rite of spring that would draw thousands of runners and over a million spectators, an audience that is the largest in the world for a sporting event.

Hundreds of reporters would check its progress, and television cameras would keep their silent, roving eyes ready to pounce for instant drama, the combustible moments that attend every big and classic event. There was only one match-up in a marathon: distance and men. But new dimensions had been added to that pure confrontation as this Boston Marathon neared: man against man and the cloaked expectation of a new frontier in time—a two-hour marathon.

It was eight A.M. when the first vendor set up his T-shirt stand on Commonwealth Avenue.

Chewing on a cigar, the man held up a shirt in front of his eyes. He looked through his smoke and studied his product. He liked its color tones, its theme: three runners nearly abreast and straining for the lead.

Franz Overbeck was out of bed now, sitting at the room-service breakfast table with Mueller. They listened to a tape deck playing Beethoven's Fifth. It was the only superstition, the one bow to luck before a big marathon that Franz always allowed himself. Later, he would turn the music up and let it crash through the room and into his mind. But now the music was distant, and his thoughts were on Greta, out in the city somewhere, planning, waiting for him after two long years.

He had come to grips with a decision during the night, had formed a private strategy that would give him both victory and Greta. The athlete in him, his reputation, his gratitude to his country—no matter how paled by Otto Al-

brecht—could not just let him hand the race to Roy Holt
and the Americans. He was not worried about the Japanese.
His plan hinged on one thing: running Holt into the
ground going up and down Heartbreak Hill, building such
a big lead going into Coolidge Corner that a Holt victory
would be compromised.

But how big of a lead? Twenty, forty, eighty yards? He
reckoned that it had to be at least a quarter-mile. With that
kind of margin, that deep into the race, there would be no
doubt about the unofficial victor; way ahead of Holt, Franz
Overbeck had left the race to defect to America and his
wife; had he stayed in the race—so the sentiment would go
—he would have won easily, for he had never broken down
at the end of a marathon in his career. He would be the
story of the day—not Roy Holt, who would have been
snuffed out so subtly before his own crowd.

Two trainers and a doctor came into the room. Franz
rolled up his sleeve, and the doctor gave him several vitamin
shots. One of the trainers gave him the morning *Globe*.
There were three big pictures on the front page: himself,
the Japanese and Holt. The East German did not bother to
read the story but passed it over to Kurt Mueller, who read
English better. Franz went back to his breakfast, shooting
questions at the trainers. With any other runner the trainers
would now be dictating the style of race. Franz devised his
own tactics.

"Everything ready?" Franz asked. "You know where
you have to be?"

"We know," said one of the trainers.

"I want the sugar solution going up Heartbreak. And
then coming down. Also, give me some sugar cubes that I
can slip under my tongue. Keep the water coming, too. It's
going to be a hard race."

Mueller slapped the paper with the back of his hand. "Holt and his two-hour barrier! He's crazy."

"Is he talking about it?" Franz asked.

"No, but the press is. They know he's not here just to win."

"Just to win?" said Franz. "Do they think he's going to win?"

"Well, he's never lost here," Mueller said.

"He loses today," Franz said.

"Don't let him draw you into his pace," said one of the trainers. "Run your own race."

"I know what I'm doing," Franz said.

The doctor moved another needle toward his arm. Franz said, "What's this?"

"A final steroid," the doctor replied.

Franz pulled his arm away. "Enough. I've had enough of those for weeks now."

"It's for your own good," Mueller said.

"Let me be the judge of that, Kurt."

"Easy," Mueller said.

"Everything's so close," Franz said. "Your people have been all over me here. You won't let me breathe. Right now, there's seven of your men out there in the living room. What's up?"

"Nothing," Kurt said.

Kurt turned back to his paper, his mind assembling the details of the day's operation. The helicopter rental had been taken care of and was waiting for his men. He looked over at the black bag on his bed containing the device that would detonate the helicopter. Everyone knew their positions. The tension began to crawl up the back of his neck. He raised his eyes toward Franz. He looked calm enough, thought Kurt.

The doctor and the trainers left, and Kurt said, "Why, Franz?"

"Why?" asked Franz.

"Why are we here?"

"For the country. Because it's a big race. And like I said before, I belong here."

"It's not too late, Franz. Let's say you've hurt your foot. Let's go home. Get out of here. Who needs it?"

"Are you crazy?"

"Yes. For being here. I never wanted to come."

Franz tossed his napkin on to the table. He walked over to Kurt and grabbed his hand. He wanted to thank him for his friendship, wanted to say he was sorry because Kurt had to be here.

"Relax," Franz said. "The day belongs to us."

Roy Holt had turned the lights on in his room, but he still sat looking at the window curtains. He hated himself for this charade, this falling into the trap. He knew enough about his fear by now to know that it always began with little things, and suddenly you were caught in the rut of in-decision—then a panic. He had heard the weather report before going to bed; but he never trusted Boston weather.

He bounced quickly out of bed and made for the window. He ripped the curtains back with both hands. For one brief second, all that he had been and hoped for on this day seemed to be hooked up to the opening of the curtains. He was ready to curse when his face broke into a smile. Rain sprayed the window. There was not a trace of sun, no melt-ing gold to slow his body. It was a beautiful day—for Jack the Ripper and marathoners.

He left the window, picked up the phone and ordered

black coffee and French toast. He went over to the bureau and began to mix his solution, a compound of water, glucose and salt. Later, he would give the bottles to Soldier Burns, who would have someone hand them to Roy on the run at vital points in the race. He didn't need anybody else, he thought. He liked being alone. No one had any chains on him; he had no motivation for being a part of any kind of word that had *-ation* or *-ology* or *ism* at the end of it.

He walked back to the window. The rain was still there. He looked down and could see the finish line of the race in the Prudential Center. He was ready to go back mixing his solution when he saw two figures moving out of the rolling mist below. He had seen them for the last three mornings: Kanji Sato and the immense sumo wrestler just staring out from the finish line to the top of the stretch.

With the gaze of an impassive Buddha, Ichy studied the two small fried eggs on his plate, then looked up at the room-service waiter. Kanji walked by the table and noticed the eggs. He told the waiter: "Bring him up three more orders." Kanji had already eaten a big breakfast but now he sat down and had some coffee.

"A black ball ran rolling into the pitch-black night," said Kanji. "Have you figured it out yet?"

"No," said Ichy.

Kanji said, "When I keep thinking about it Rai's face is right next to me. It is like he is with me."

Ichy said, "It is damp today."

"Yes," Kanji said. "I've been feeling cold all morning."

"No sun. You wanted sun."

"I always like to race with the sun on me," Kanji said.

"You are ready," Ichy said.

"I have never felt better. The road ends here, Ichy. The past and the present become united."

"A dozen newspaper men. Two television crews. The radio people. Just from Japan alone."

"The whole nation will live every mile," Kanji said. "I am going to have my day."

Kanji got up, coffee in hand, and walked to the window. Down at the finish line, the Japanese students from Harvard were setting up the huge drums, ceremonial drums that they would pound in teams from the start of the race to the finish. Beating the drums with stumps, the students would be trying to transmit a primitive energy to Kanji.

"Those drums and the blade," Kanji said. "That's all I will see and hear. No Roy Holt. No East German."

Ichy moved his slits of eyes toward Kanji. "If you cannot reach this two-hour barrier, promise me you will not feel bad. Or defeated. As long as you win. That will matter."

The words passed by Kanji. "Japanese have won here before," he said.

He went to the closet, put on a long white kimono, and began to lay out his running clothes: elbow-length white gloves and red and white shoes, the same colors for his running jacket, race pants and tank top. The light top and jacket carried the same emblems: ideographs on the front near the heart and a rising sun flaming on the back. The ideographs denoted the numbers ten and one put together, the samurai symbol for ten conflicting impulses blended into the state of single concentration. The rising sun was the spirit of Japan.

He then went over to the Shinto altar on the coffee table. Next to the altar were pictures of the two spirits that divided his heart and had driven him here to the supreme moment of his life: his father Yatero and his great-grandfather

Takamori; the banker and the warlord-hero. He lit three sticks of incense, watched the smoke wreath the altar, then unsheathed Takamori's ancient sword, standing it straight up in front of the altar. He watched the light sparkle off the blade, then slowly, ever so slowly, began to breathe and let the *ki-ai* seep into his body of perfect posture.

Eighty-six years before, a man had taken a stick and drawn a line across a dusty road in Ashland, a little town west of Boston. Pastoral and a long way from the big city back then, the town with the line across Main Street had been the starting place for the first Boston Marathon. Fifteen runners, wearing heavy boots and pants, took off for Boston, and twenty-four miles later (the distance then) the winner was an Irish bartender named John J. McDermott. He did the course in two hours, fifty-five minutes and ten seconds. Devastated and reflective, he said he would settle back to being a man of imprecise morals.

Now, with five minutes before noon showing on the church clock in Ashland, an energized mass of humanity buzzed its way to the blacktop of Main Street. The field was enormous: over six thousand runners, men and women from every stratum of American life, each with his own private reasons for going against the distance. They would dig at the course for hours with a gray persistence until they finished. There were no rewards. Except maybe a line of agate type in the next day's paper. They were the gritty backbone of the Boston Marathon.

Shoulder to shoulder, heads bobbing, the thousands of bodies stretched back as far as the eye could see. The whole town had a certain feel: of nervous sweat, of tiny fears; it was the look of a horse in full lather. The horde shuffled in place now, their faces wet from the fine rain, as the band began to play the Japanese, East German and American anthems. From high above, off to the left, a helicopter dipped languidly in the leaden, scudding clouds.

The band slogged on, limping tinnily through the foreign anthems, then zooming full-blown into "The Star-Spangled Banner." Some of the runners tried to edge their way through the tangle of bodies to the front; it was useless, there could be no justice for all here. After the gun, it might be a half hour before the last runners in the pack crossed the starting line. The top hundred runners—by past performance—bided their time in a roped rectangle at the nose of the mass, ending in a tip where three runners stood: Franz Overbeck, Kanji Sato and Roy Holt, part of the reason why half of Boston was now waiting along every inch of the miles ahead.

For two weeks, the press and the people had defined the event: country against country, reputation against reputation; the plutocratic image of the marathon as religion had now joined the commonwealth of sport. The sheaths of stories had not missed an angle: the running sword, the subway samurai in a three-piece suit that was the Japanese; the model of East German science, the handsome Aryan who had given up a wife for an ideal; and the driven American who might once more throw himself on the spikes of the impossible—a two-hour marathon.

The figures and styles backed up the colorful prose. Kanji Sato: a man of pure and dazzling speed who held the world marathon record with two hours three minutes. Franz Overbeck: all strength and cunning, a proud man who had never lost a race in his life—except to Holt up in Montreal. And Roy Holt: power, speed and daring, winner of three straight Boston Marathons and holder of the world record for the ten thousand meters with twenty-seven minutes fifteen seconds.

Holt was the first to see the gun come out of the starter's pocket. He caught the German's eye, smiled and motioned for him to be ready. Franz ignored him and took a deep breath. Roy turned his eyes to Sato. The Japanese stood erect, hardly breathing, his face blank, his own eyes ridged with Vaseline like a fighter coming out for the first round. A squad of butterflies tickled his throat, and he chased them back to his stomach.

Quiet. Just the low drone of the waving line of thousands in the rear. Then the single clap of the gun, freeing a long hiss as if a drum of oil had been punctured. The long trail of bone and muscle oozed out of Hopkinton, 26 miles and 385 yards away from Boston and the finish line in the mesa of the Prudential Center, where office workers would be hanging out of windows and the area would be walled by fans. Where a merciless digital clock—hanging up there like a technological bug—would be the final arbiter of men against distance.

Cracking into the first half-mile, the trio of Sato, Holt and Overbeck left the thunder of the pack behind them. They moved up and down, mostly down, with quick twists past cottages and woods and walls of stacked stone, until they were out on Route 135 and moving past an old clock factory in Ashland, causing Roy to glance at his wristwatch and review his pace. *Pace! Pace! Pace!* He couldn't let himself forget it, he thought, looking ahead at the streaking Kanji Sato. Roy felt light and loose. The butterflies were gone, and his time of four minutes twenty-eight seconds for that first mile was right on the nose.

With slight variation, the three stayed in that lineup for the next four miles: Kanji clamped to a thirty-yard lead; Roy hard by his 4:30 pace; and Franz ten yards behind the American. There were two trucks in front of Kanji, one a mobile unit for television, the other filled with photographers stacked up like beer cans. This was the best time in the marathon, so distant from all the minus factors: the body heat that could rise as high as 106; the dehydration from water loss of as much as five liters or more, depending on the pace; the terrible pain in the legs and chest; the loss of eye focus; the agony of Heartbreak Hill.

Heartbreak was the voodoo magic of the Boston Marathon, a physical reality for many good runners although a myth to most world-class men, who saw it only as a psychological mirage to be handled with strength and will. But it would be real enough for most of those back in the pack, and long before that hill was in view they would sense the infamous wall of pain that was waiting, that would suck the last sugar from their bodies and leave them like slain flowers on its rise and crest. The wall did not interest Roy. He had his own demon, and he knew where it lived—inside the pace and dehydration of the last five miles.

Roy noticed the crowd as they slipped over the train tracks at Framingham, a little over six and a half miles into the race. He was startled as Kanji nearly ran over the fans. There had never been a crowd like this in Framingham. He had always been used to open space here. But there was not much running room, and he wondered what it was going to be like when they hit Boston. Still on his 4:30 pace, Roy kept his eyes on the flaming red ball, the rising sun on Kanji's back. Just keep him in sight, thought Roy. He did not bother to look back at the East German. He knew where he was, ten yards off his left flank, right where he would be most of the race, aware that Holt knew every turn in the course, just hanging out there like a prairie hawk, all eyes and ears—waiting. Roy slowed and grabbed his solution from an official: water, glucose and salt.

Natick: ten and a half miles into the course. An East German trainer ran next to Franz with a bottle of liquid B-15 vitamin, a distillation of many experiments and high belief in Moscow and Leipzig. Franz took several swallows.

"The American is sound," Franz said, still running. "He hasn't moved off his pace." The trainer handed him a green bottle.

"The Japanese," said the trainer, trying to stay with him. "Well under 4:30."

Franz drained the bottle through a straw. "He won't last."

"Stay with them," said the trainer.

"Am I going to walk?" Franz said, showing his contempt for the trainer's inane words. He then pulled away.

Rocking and swerving above him, the helicopter now gave Franz some lead line.

The spotter said, "He just drank."

"Is he running well?" asked Mueller in the car on the ground, the detonator primed and on the front seat.

"Beautiful," the spotter said.

"Good! Good!" Mueller answered. Franz was not running like a man who had something on his mind.

"So many runners," said the spotter. "Thousands stretched out for miles behind the leaders."

"Keep on top of him," Mueller said.

The man with the rifle aimed, bringing Franz's back into his cross-hair sight.

"What are you doing?" the spotter asked.

"Just practicing."

"Put that down," the spotter said, with a sour look.

Nine miles to the hill, thought Franz. He looked ahead at Holt, loping with grace and sureness. He seemed to be stronger, more thrusting than in Ethiopia. He thought back to how the American had handled the downhill on that terrain. You had to take the measure of the American on hills; you couldn't chance fooling with him on the flat. He recalled how he had worked Holt more than six months before, pushing up the red hills, then whipping him on the downside. The American's legs were too long for the downhill rigor. He did not have the musculature to handle the shock, to provide the control for steep descent. He could hold his own; that was all. He would leave Holt tangled in his feet coming down Heartbreak.

His pace, thought Franz. It was steady, perfect like a fine Swiss watch, a hypnotic repetition that impressed Franz with its discipline. Was Holt trying to lure him into some subtle trap, hoping that it would bluff him into anxiety? If Holt knew anything about him at all, it was that Franz Overbeck could never be distracted. No, the American was working his own strange gauntlet, playing carefully around the edges of his consuming passion—a two-hour marathon. Franz saw himself as the benevolent executioner who, with one mighty swing of his ax, would release the grip of that delusion.

Roy saw the blue and gold banner stretched across Natick, looked down the narrow lane defined by the crowd and caught a glimpse of Kanji scooting under the banner forty yards ahead. Roy listened to the chant of the crowd. *Holt! Holt! Holt!* The fans wanted him to go after Kanji. The little man out there in front, the rhythm of the chanting was seductive. But he'd blow it all if he tried to run over Kanji now. Who was this man? Where was the ballast within him for such an effort? Tradition? Honor? That was the story of him in the press. Words. He'd like to have a look at his face, to look for the fine lines of pain, to listen to his breath, measure the depth of the man. He looked up at the sky. The dark clouds rolled over each other swiftly. Even the sky was running today, he thought.

Never looking over his shoulder, Kanji was tucked in front of the press trucks. The crowd just gaped at the short, bullet-headed figure in white gloves up to his elbows, so fluid for a runner with bowed legs, now whirling like spokes on a wickedly engineered bicycle. Kanji kept his black eyes drilled into space. His face was devoid of strain, free of emotion, more like the somber, painted figurehead of a clipper ship trained on the horizon, the next roll of the sea. The crowd loosed a roar as he passed, a sound of respect and disappointed awe.

"It's the Jap's race today," said one fan.

"He might as well be in a Toyota," said another.

"Roy'll nail him," said another voice. "Nobody beats Holt in this race."

"Here he comes now!" said a burly man with a kid on his shoulders. "The Commie's right with him."

"Forget it," said the first man again. "It's the Jap's race today."

Kanji opened up a sixty-yard lead, shooting down a long gradual slope that crossed the Natick-Wellesley line, past the martini parties on lawns behind low, stone walls. There was no clock in his head, no ground beneath him. He was as remote from his body as he had been in the room full of mosquitoes. There was only a block of steel on an anvil in his mind, glowing and sparking as hammers pounded it into flatness until the layers were fused over and over into each other.

Wellesley College: thirteen and a half miles from Hopkinton, halfway to the finish. Over six hundred girls now lined the route, their hair blowing in the wind, their breasts jiggling as they jumped and cheered, caught up in the festival mood of this rite of seasonal change that promised them warm sun and beaches so very soon. But the leaders were no fun; there was an intense sobriety to them that reminded them of dreary classes, the pressure of winning and losing in exams. The extreme back of the pack would be much more to their liking: the bent old men shuffling along, the young men and women with suffering on their faces who would be thankful for a pretty smile and a cup of water thrown on their hot bodies.

Roy dodged a cup of water, chased an image of his dead wife, Amy, from his mind and drilled his mind to the pace: ninety minutes to Heartbreak Hill, four minutes thirty seconds a mile. He had gone over the pace by seconds on a couple of miles but had undercut it on several others; on schedule, Roy slowed for more liquid.

Twenty yards in back now, Franz eased his stride for his own solution while watching the helicopter above him, still quite high; he left part of his vision on the American. He could see some method in Holt's refueling. He had taken the liquid four times already, was coasting on his 4:30 pace until the sugar began to course through his body, then would knife into a brilliant pattern of speed for three quarters of a mile before moving back to his old pace. He had done his work for this race, thought Franz. The man was fit, of a finely welded piece. He had thought Holt had lost his mettle; somewhere he had gotten it back—for now.

Four more miles, and the trio glided through Auburndale, with Kanji now working on a hundred-yard lead, trailed by Roy, and Franz running third, thirty yards back. The crowd was more vocal, emotional here as it cluttered the lane and pushed in on Roy. The people were waving American flags; he'd never seen that before in this race. They were not runners anymore. They were countries, locked into some vague, undeclared war that only the people here seemed to sense.

The mood was foreign to Roy. They were only athletes who punished their bodies, their psyches, followed tenets known only to those who had ever tried to live up to them. This stage, insisting on a display of national character, festooned with banners and signs and charged with the sound of trumpets, made him feel uneasy; it seemed more virulent than the atmosphere at an Olympics. For a moment. Then, oddly, it began to buoy him, to send the adrenaline through his body, though he knew he had no nationalistic anger in him. He couldn't think of nations, or the man in front or in back of him. He was concentrating on two other enemies: dehydration and fear of the Oslo aftermath.

Fists clenched, the crowd sang: "Go! Go! Go! Go! Go!"

"Lemme through!" yelled Roy. "Gimme . . . gimme room!"

"Don't let 'im take you, Roy!"

"I can't see! Where is he?" He kept shouting the words as the crowd opened up before him. He moved into the clear and glanced back at Overbeck. He didn't want him getting caught in the snare back there. The East German was not slowing up. Hands reached out for him, and Overbeck whipped his arms out like scythes to clear the way. He churned and bulled his way through the crowd, then came out forty yards behind the American. He was not ruffled or angry. He simply pressed a button and let his mind coil around the moment he had been waiting for, that point of final reckoning less than three miles away: Heartbreak Hill.

After a little over eighteen miles, the malevolent formation loomed in the distance, a no-man's reef of lost ships for Boston runners. Like sea tales whispered in faraway ports of another time, the exotica of Heartbreak's terror grew with each new fallen body. If the spent minds and bodies, their wills mangled, their systems empty of sugar, their last body fat simmering to a crisp, were to be laid end to end, the victims over the years would cover the whole distance of the marathon. Heartbreak was a three-block, six-hundred yard fifty-degree gradient, past quiet old homes with tree-shaded verandas carrying signs that said "Rest."

It was thought that Heartbreak was not the toughest of hills, the highest or steepest in world marathons, yet all agreed that its location was the most diabolical, coming at that precise time when body and spirit were at their lowest ebb; a jolt of surprise even for old hands, it was like a cinder flying into your eye on a clear, windless day. Here was a dual threat: the hill and the cruel wall of bodily resistance that was thrown up in every marathon at the twenty-mile limit. That was where so many had stopped running and started walking, dropped to one knee, wobbled down to oblivion.

But runners like Holt and Overbeck recognized no wall; the book was still out on Kanji; so far, he looked like he was going to smash everything in front of him. Roy had respect for Heartbreak; he would work it today as he always had. Some runners attacked it with a dagger between their teeth, others ran with wariness or let the hill intimidate them out of their strategy. Roy had learned to blend into it, to use control and not be frustrated and to come away from it intact. He knew it would exact its price, toss the climb at him like an old bill near the finish—but not now; the hill was only a hill.

Looking at the hill, Franz cut his speed for more liquid; he trailed Holt by thirty yards now.

"Soon," Franz said.

"What?" the trainer said.

"I'll leave the American on the hill now."

"Be careful," the trainer said. "It is tricky."

"Shut up!" Franz yelled.

His future was on this hill: the whole race and Greta. She was waiting. Just four miles away.

Roy made his approach to Heartbreak. Kanji was already moving up the hill. Roy looked for a wobble. Nothing. A head that was weary and rolling loosely as if it were broken. Nothing. He started to turn back to Overbeck. Too late. The East German was right next to him and booming to the front. Roy stayed with his pace and braked slightly for the liquid, which was now being extended by a puffing Soldier Burns, his legs trying to keep up with Roy.

"The Jap's takin' that hill like it's a curb!" Soldier shouted.

"You see his face?" Roy asked.

"Like it's frozen!"

"I'll be at the hill. On time."

"Figure eighty-nine minutes."

"One minute under. Beautiful."

"Forget two hours, son. Win this goddamn race!"

Roy dug into the pace again. He knew he'd lose time over the hill, had figured it into his plan. He wanted a 4:50 pace over the hill and the next mile and a half. That would bring him out on Lake Street. Now he began his climb up Heartbreak.

The man sat in back of the pilot with his rifle across his lap and listened to the voice in his headset. The helicopter hovered over Heartbreak.

"Nothing," said the spotter in the front seat.

"Where are you now?" Mueller asked from the ground.

"The hill. Franz is gaining quickly now on the Japanese. I've never seen him run like this."

"Wonderful," Mueller said. "This is all for nothing."

"The curare is in the rifle," the gunner said.

"Be calm!" Mueller shouted. "You listen to the spotter! Do you hear me!"

The sound of the word "curare" made Kurt tremble. He could see the dart shapes, the points smeared with curare. No pain. The poison would be carried by the blood from the wound through the body. His arms, his legs would become heavy, he would want to close his eyes, but the lids would suddenly be of iron. He would want to scream. The tongue would lie leaden. He would hear and see everything. The drying of his mouth and eyes would bring some pain. He would sit down, then fall to one side. He could do nothing to help himself. He would be in a state where he could be cut to pieces, his chest opened up and the heart action observed. The gunner up there would aim for the spinal column. His friend would be dead in five minutes. Kurt thought: Run! Run! Run! Let us go home together!

Listening to the radio in the car, Big Smith sat behind the wheel just off Coolidge Corner and said, "He'll be coming soon, Greta. Be happy." She said nothing.

They were parked about twenty yards off the course. Up front, two cops had cleared a path through the crowd and up to the car.

"I'll say this for him," Little Smith said, sitting in back. "Your husband is murder out there today."

"It's a brutal race," Big Smith said.

"That is Franz's life out there," Greta said.

Big said, "He's running like he's not going to quit in a few miles."

"Be quiet, will ya?" Little said. "Don't rattle her."

"He knows no other way to run," Greta said, looking straight ahead at the patch of clearing on the course.

Halfway up the hill, Roy saw Franz wash over the Japanese on the crest. He had watched them both going up Heartbreak, impressed by the East German's calves bulging like cannonballs, his heels high off the road, pulling the hill back under him and throwing it into Roy's face. Why was he so frantic here, so desperate to make a move? He knew better. Is he trying to spook me? thought Roy. What of Kanji? Had he cut his speed, or was he finished?

Roy pounded his way up Heartbreak, feeling the pain now in the back of his legs. The dunes! The dunes! Keep your mind on the dunes! They had been meaner than this hill, and so was the old Buck, who had been on top of them, cursing, kneeling up there and hammering his fists in the sand for more, more and still more. He could see Buck's face, crooked and mocking, and now Roy was at the top and he ran right over his veined nose.

The best hill runner in the world, the East German took a ten-yard lead over the Japanese as he neared the base of Heartbreak. He gave a quick look over his shoulder to check the American's position. Holt was just starting his descent, right where Franz wanted him to be, ensnarled in the downhill. He broke now for Lake Street, running right by his trainer with the liquid. Silent, startled, the crowd watched Franz accelerate by them as if he had never been on their killing Heartbreak Hill. Franz looked back again. Holt wasn't in sight. Kanji was twenty yards behind. He didn't care about him. His rendezvous at Coolidge Corner was now only two and a half miles away.

Roy hit the base of Heartbreak, grabbed a bottle of liquid from an official and began the first of his big moves. He had come off the hill—as he had figured—with only a small piece of himself left there. He had run Heartbreak better than at any time in his career. The work—up and down so many times—in the soft sand of that dune had tuned his legs perfectly. Now he was ready to push closer to the two-hour barrier. He slammed into a 4:30 pace, thinking: Take that speed into Coolidge Corner and then blow it out no matter where it leaves you, whether in a pool of black vomit or in a lifetime of nightmares.

Soon he was breasting Kanji, with a mile and a half to go to Coolidge Corner. There was no hurt on the little man's face. His breathing was shallow. Kanji had clearly cut back on his speed. He had cut a spectacular pace of 4:30 or so from the start. He probably knew now, thought Roy, that he couldn't wire this field. Or was he saving something, holding back some last measure of searing speed to hurl at Holt and Overbeck? He looked again at his face. Empty. He passed by him, and now he could see Overbeck, sixty yards in front.

Franz heard the crowd erupt behind him. He didn't look back. He knew the roar was for Holt. Who else? Franz's powerful drive for a quarter-mile lead into Coolidge Corner hadn't unnerved the American. The hill hadn't devoured him. Why had he ever thought it would; had he played some absurd trick on himself, been harpooned by his own muddy thinking? His ego, his pride, had never given Holt credit, though he had always heard the dire whispers of his unconscious. The American seemed to be forever like an eerie guide to his fate; now he was forcing him into the decision of his life.

He looked back at Holt. Franz's lead was evaporating; Kanji was behind Holt by twenty yards—with less than a mile to Coolidge Corner. The speed was being drawn out of Franz by his own indecision. He cursed the American. Love? Was there such a thing? Or had he just felt sorry for himself? Could a wife's love compare with that of a whole nation, or its confidence in him? The admiration of his peers. The worship of the young. The looks of pride on the Leipzig streets. The idea of betrayal jarred him.

Confusion flooded over him. He thought of the elk

standing on the rock in the Harz Mountains, its tree of antlers sparkling in the sun. Defiant. Free. Like Greta. Albrecht's face was there now, his bluish lips moving: "Whore! Whore! The rotten seed of a hundred men!" The ventriloquist. And the dummy who would not speak. The mental pain of that moment made him wince. He deserved more, and so did Greta. He needed room for living. He wasn't a nation. Just a man.

A quarter of a mile to Greta. He must think fast. The hard thumb on his life had been costly. Willy dead. Greta gone. And more to come if he took the turn at Coolidge Corner: Kurt Mueller's career in ruins, his lovely family at bay; Heinrich just a knock on the door from prison or death. The weight was too much. Even though he knew his defection would wreck Otto, the power and the man, would cause a cracking rumble to snake through the Institute and the Federation. Do it! Don't do it! He cursed himself for his weakness, his failure to handle a single act of conviction. He berated himself: "You've never had a thought of your own in your entire life."

Franz was in a daze. His mind was off the race. He could see Coolidge Corner up ahead. He could hear Holt in the rear, ten yards or so to the left. Roy drew closer. The East German's smooth gait was broken. He seemed baffled, hesitant. Then, like a match being struck, Franz kicked and peeled out in front of Holt, shooting to the left of the course.

The helicopter dropped from the sky.

"He is going!" shouted the spotter into the radio. He screamed to the pilot, "Down! Down! Closer!" The helicopter swooped and swayed over Franz.

"No! No!" cried Kurt from the ground. Beads of sweat popped out on his forehead.

"He's going!"

Kurt's finger twitched above the black device that would blow up the men and the helicopter. "Oh, my God!" he said.

"It's a woman!" said the spotter. "It's her! His wife! They're off to the side."

"Right below me!" said the gunner. "Perfect!"

The gunner raised his weapon. He moved the sight down Franz's back, drawing his finger on the trigger.

"Keep it still!" shouted the gunner.

Franz shot for the opening in the crowd.

The East German felt the helicopter tightening down on him. He saw Greta clearly now, the long, yellow hair, her clenched fists. He could feel the blades above him whipping a violent wind over his hot body and through his wet hair. He jerked his head toward the sky. The American was to his right and moving out now. He looked once more at Greta. Holt was in his peripheral vision, his turning legs like beckoning hands, luring and pulling him back to his life, to the race, to the basics that define any athlete: character and self-esteem. He could not ignore who and what he was, turn his back on the nature of the breed. He and Holt were building a work of art here today. He would claim it as his own.

Franz swerved and fired past Coolidge Corner. The whine of the helicopter drowned his cry.

"*Nein! Nein, Greta!*"

And then he was gone.

* * *

191

The finger dropped off the rifle's trigger. The copter swayed and darted for the open sky.

"He didn't go," the spotter said quietly.

"Thank God!" Mueller yelled, wiping his brow, pulling his finger quickly away from the button. Exhausted, he slumped back in his car seat.

Greta saw her husband's face for only a few seconds. She started to run, stopped, then dashed out to the street. Kanji nearly ran her over. She dropped to her knees and gazed emptily up the course as Franz took off after the American.

"The ungrateful bastard!" Little Smith said, lifting her by the elbows.

"The system," Greta said softly. "The Institute. He can't change."

"I knew he wasn't running a race he was going to quit," Little Smith said.

"Bullshit!" Big Smith yelled, coming out after talking on the car radio. "You see the rifle? It was hanging out of the copter. They were going to snuff him!"

"But I didn't . . ." Greta started to say.

"Let's go!" Big Smith bellowed. "We got some business at the finish."

Thousands of eyes stayed on the pulsating digits on the big clock at the finish line in the Prudential Center.

The PA system echoed through the mesa of glass and steel.

"Time: two miles to the finish, one hour, fifty-eight minutes and 48 seconds."

The crowd groaned. The PA system listed the leaders.

Holt was out in front. The roar rattled the windows. The East German was second. Kanji Sato was third.

The primitive sound of the Japanese drums grew in decibels.

A pale sun squirmed out of the sky.

Nine minutes for two miles, thought Roy, hitting Kenmore Square, keeping an eye on some people holding buckets of water. He didn't want any water splashed on him; let them save it for the back of the pack. He looked at his watch. He was trying to stay at a 4:30 pace yet couldn't. His pace was slowing. The sub-4:35 from the bottom of Heartbreak past Coolidge Corner had drained him. He began to feel nausea as he hit the broad, malled boulevard of Commonwealth Avenue. It was becoming blurred, a waving vista of old brick, the filigree of wrought iron, grand old town houses with prismed windows, a parade of oaken doors with big, brass knockers. Hundreds of people were standing on the roofs, and the sky rained balloons and a chorus that now seemed weird to his ears: "TWO! TWO! TWO! TWO! TWO!"

Ten yards back, Franz Overbeck popped three cubes of sugar. Greta might as well have been a figure in a fantasy. He concentrated all his attention on the American, lining him up for the kill and admiring him at the same time. Holt had built this stage for him today, and now the two-hour marathon, the Institute's "death race," was no longer a myth or the dark force of one man's impossible quest. How could he have ever thought of turning off back there, of not being the dominant figure in this masterpiece of speed and distance? There would be no death here—only life. He heard the slap of Kanji's feet behind him. He saw the American wobble. Now!

Roy was stung by the rush of Overbeck and Sato. They were both by him now. Sensuous and comforting, a tender hug of euphoria reached around his body and mind, easing the sting, slowing the contraction of his muscles. The caring, sensitive voice welled up through the chamber: *Easy, Roy, you're tired, so tired, you're going to kill yourself out here—and for what?* The voice should not have asked. For what! Why! Why! Always why! *So you're a hero. Nobody cares.* Because I care, goddamn it, I care! *Good, you win the sucker's prize. Remember Oslo! New Zealand. You were sensible in New Zealand. Coast home. Be nice to yourself, Roy.*

Cold ran through his body, gooseflesh broke out on his stomach and chest. His skin felt cool and clammy. It was here: dehydration. The jockey has the rail that he really doesn't want any part of on a thousand-pound, spooky horse. The fighter has the chin that cracks like a cheap wineglass, or the opponent's right hand that he knows will be there and can't ever pick off. Footsteps for the wide receiver, a white ninety-mile-per-hour blur at the head of a baseball hitter. Dehydration: the curse of a torrid pace.

Just a little further. The liquid stop. The hand of the official moved up and down like the hand of a skeleton. Everything was quiet. As if he was the last man in the world. He saw a parked car rise up on dinosaur legs and rush toward him. He was there now, tearing the bottle of sugar and water out of the official's hand. The liquid snaked down through his throat. He could hear the crowd now. A balloon bobbed in front of him.

Once more, he tried to bring the leaders into focus.

Less than a mile to go. He had lost all sense of time and

pace and was running on automatic pilot. The East German was still ahead, two lengths now in front of Kanji. Roy was twenty-five yards off the lead. He had to be closer when they turned into Hereford Street. Fright pounded up through him, tearing at his head. He was sliding on his belly through black vomit and bloody urine. *Give it up*, came the chamber voice. The other words came now: *Shut up, you whimpering punk! You're not afraid of death!* The liquid began to fire his muscles. Sweat finally broke through his clammy skin. He took a bead on the leaders, the hoarse plea of Buck Lewis crashing through his eardrums: *Second wind! Second wind!*

It was the invisible elixir that propels the body of all great athletes and men who face physical or mental fatigue. Ordinary words to kids in the playground, to flabby men who remember competition, jock talk for boardroom martinets. Few—sometimes not even those who had it—recognized it for what it was: a phenomenon, first advanced by William James, brother of Henry, pioneer in psychology. But Buck knew its truth: men were lazy, prisoners of limits, habitually inclined to surrender to fatigue by degrees. How often had they talked about it, Buck saying: Man has no limits.

Stay with me, Buck, thought Roy, don't leave me now. He could hear Buck now: *You're on your own, Roy. Bust through. Hold back, give in now, and you'll spend the rest of your life as damaged goods to yourself, a piano with soundless ivories, a violin with the strings attached only at one end; nobody else will know—but you will.* Roy could hear the throb through the long tunnel of people: NOW! NOW! NOW! NOW!

They turned onto Hereford Street, a narrow, teeming conduit that led up to a turn at Boylston Street, and then

195

the unpardoning eye of the clock in the Prudential Center. Heat. Haze. Hereford was like running into a dark cave with clusters of hanging bats squealing and ready to drop and wing into your face. Franz was still on the point, Kanji four lengths back, and Roy had closed the gap to ten yards. Water was flying out of the windows of the row houses. Roy saw a kid with a bucket of water, and he waved the bucket toward his face. Now he wanted the coolness. The kid whipped the water into his pale-flushed skin.

And now they started into the second block of row houses on Hereford. Roy was gaining. The East German seemed to be bending to his right. Probably a belly cramp, thought Roy; Franz was in pain. Kanji was on Franz's heels. People were hanging out of windows and spraying confetti. The runners could now hear the swollen, continuous roar rising up from the finish line around the corner. Then a shower of water fell on Franz and Kanji, and Roy couldn't believe the scene in front of him: Kanji stopped. He just stopped and raised his fists to the sky. Roy was now next to him, the words driving up through him.

"Don't quit now!" Roy yelled. "Not now!"

Kanji stood frozen, looking as if he didn't know where he was. Roy could see the fury in the little man's eyes, then the panic as if a vital substance had been sucked out of him. The water ran down his face and squeaked in his shoes. Kanji wanted to scream in rage. All eyes were on him. Kanji's sword was in a thousand pieces, broken steel on the ground at his feet. His concentration, his *ki-ai* energy-trickled out of his mind and belly. He pivoted sharply and ran back into the race, trying desperately to rebuild the *ki-ai* that had been loosed by his anger.

Roy was well past Kanji now, and only four yards in

back of Franz at the end of the row houses. He could sense Kanji once more behind him. He had only stopped for a few seconds. But how long was a second? A day, a week, a year, a lifetime? He had no sense of time. They began their turn on Boylston Street. Franz swept wide, still leaning to his right. Roy shot inside for the imaginary rail. He saw the face of Franz, his mouth wide open and gulping air, his eyes feral and bloodshot.

Roy hit the top of the stretch dead even with Franz and saw and heard it all only once—and just barely: the reflection of sun and steel, people on roofs or like tiny birds in office windows, wall-to-wall people held back by the cops; the tribal booming of the Japanese drums, the massive cataract of sound: TWO! TWO! TWO! TWO! TWO! The giant digital bug blinked: 1:59:34 . . . 1:59:37 . . . 1:59:40. He and Franz were shoulder to shoulder, Kanji three yards back.

Roy looked to his right. Franz was weaving out to his right, sliding back sideways and then out again. Roy went for the jugular, the ground no longer under his own feet. He heard a faint cry behind him from Kanji: Aaaaaaaaaaaeeeeeeeeee! Kanji had reached for the red-hot poker, sent the last of his *ki-ai* toward the finish. And now there was only a ghostly silence for Roy: mouths opening and closing, a Day-Glo wash of light and a mass of people moving up and down in slow motion like horrid puppets.

They hit the finish, with Roy five strides up, their lungs bursting and sucking air, their bodies clanging, a hideous frieze of faces that would hold a place in the memory forever: mouths pulled open, the lips drawn back from the teeth in a near-snarl, the foreheads ridged over narrow eyes, the brows drawn upward; masks proving the destructive force of minds against a fixed idea—and to all eyes but those of the East German, the American and the Japanese, a pitiless and consummate vision of sorrow.

Under the ramp of the Prudential Building and in the quiet, gray recovery area, Franz stumbled into the arms of Kurt Mueller and his men.

"The time?" Franz gasped.

Mueller, his eyes moist, said, "You were superb. Your time was 2:00:02."

"Did I win?" Franz asked, his feet dragging behind him.

Mueller moved a piece of paper in front of Franz's half-closed eyes. It read: 1:59:9. "The Japanese was third," said Mueller. "In 2:00:05."

"He did it," Franz said. "The American did it." He dropped to the ground. "My God!" He buried his face in his hands.

Soldier Burns stood and watched from the ambulance, then said to a doctor: "Let's go, Doc."

Soldier moved briskly over to the kneeling Franz, who was circled by East German security.

He looked down at Franz, then at the doctor in charge of the recovery area. "What do you think, Doc?"

The doctor bent over and listened to Franz's heart with his stethoscope. The doctor looked up, shaking his head doubtfully.

"That's it!" Soldier said. "He goes to the hospital."

"We have our own doctor!" Mueller yelled.

The East German doctor said, "He is our responsibility."

"Listen!" Soldier shouted. "This is my marathon. I run it, you understand! What I say goes! This man goes to the hospital! He's sick!" He motioned for the ambulance men to bring a stretcher.

"No!" Mueller cried. He stepped in front of Soldier. The hands of his security men glided up to their chests. Mueller looked at the circle of his men and said, "Easy, now."

Soldier leveled his eyes on Mueller. "You get out of the way, or you're going to jail. Got that? We don't take chances with lives in the Boston Marathon!"

Big Smith and Little Smith came up with the stretcher. There was a long silence. "Just leave it here, boys," Soldier said, not looking at the Smiths. "The doc and me, we'll carry him over." Little Smith went back to the wheel, Big into the back of the vehicle. Soldier and Mueller stood eye to eye.

Finally, Mueller stepped aside. Soldier, gracious now, said to Mueller, "Sensible, you are. Just a checkup. You can have him back in a few hours. You can even go with him." Mueller relaxed. He started toward the closed ambulance doors. They opened, and he watched Franz being eased in. His eyes followed him, and as he looked inside he saw a flash of long corn-silk hair.

Kurt ran for the doors, reaching them just before they closed. Big Smith's heavy leg caught him in the chest, sent him reeling backward.

"Kidnapped! Kidnapped!" Mueller screamed.

Little Smith turned the siren on, and a cordon of cops eased the ambulance out of the building.

Mueller watched his career leave with Franz. He was helpless. They would all pay now: Zweig, Otto Albrecht, right up to the highest levels of the Institute and the Federation. The defection of Franz Overbeck would be a serious reversal of morale—and the impetus of East German propaganda. The government would need victims. If he was lucky, they might ignore him or bust him down to some witless function; he'd settle for it. Yes, they would be after bigger game, the source of the Boston idea: Otto Albrecht. The thought made him smile. He could see Albrecht being stripped of his power, being held in detention as if he had been in collusion with the West, then facing a ruthless board of public inquiry that would creatively decimate his past career and leave him without a future in the bureaucracy. There would only be common factory work open to him; Otto wouldn't complain; after all, they would have shot him in Russia.

Inside the ambulance, Greta kissed Franz on the cheek, then clamped an oxygen mask on his mouth. She moved her hands soothingly through his wet, blond hair.

"We made it, darling," she whispered. "We made it."

His chest heaving, his eyes flickering, Franz nodded and held her hand.

"Kidnapped?" Big Smith asked, his eyes going first to Greta, then to Franz.

"Were you kidnapped?" Greta asked.

There was a long pause. Franz moved the mask. "*Nein,*" he said.

Carried on Ichy's back up to his hotel room, Kanji Sato now lay on his bed, his eyes closed, a bottle of water in his limp hand. Ichy sat in a chair next to him.

"Water," said Ichy. "Take more water."

Kanji opened his eyes, red and vacant. "Water," he said.

"I know," said Ichy.

"An accident," said Kanji, looking at the bottle in his hand. "I beat myself."

He saw his leg digging many times into Ichy's belly the night after his father's funeral. He thought of the Jesuit's words; hysteria, rage; the ironical emotional weaknesses of a people who loved the bold surprise—but faced it with imbalance. He thought of Rai's story, of the monk who had harnessed the cancer, only to release it ten years later by stepping on a thorn.

"Please leave," said Kanji.

"No," said Ichy, sitting on the chair next to the bed.

"For a moment."

"No," said Ichy, remembering the Jesuit's words.

"Stand outside the door. Please."

Ichy rose. Kanji stared at the small Shinto altar as his friend left the room.

Putting on his robe, Kanji knelt down in front of the altar, lit the incense sticks and let his eyes fall on the pictures of his father and grandfather. The shame for his father was gone, replaced by his own deep sense of failure. He himself had built the bridge to this moment—out of pure motive and ancestral duty. There could be no retreat for him now—no honor without seppuku.

Kanji raised his grandfather's sword. He heard the distant roar of the crowd below in the Prudential Center. He thought of a haiku verse, the sort that friends send to each other before death in Japan. He fumbled in his mind for it, then it came easily. *"I sought to drive back the clouds/ With these legs sweep clear the evil stars/ But the ground within me faltered/ Who will remember this madman of Japan?"* He took the towel from around his neck, covered his hand with it, then grabbed the hilt of the sword that had known so much glory.

Kanji aimed it at his *tanden*, where he had been made a new man from the *ki-ai* energy. The long hours of practice made him think of Rai, his last farewell: *A black ball ran rolling into the pitch-black night.* How often had he thought of those words? What did they mean? He tried to chase them from his head, but they kept rushing at him along with the holy man's eyes, which seemed to shimmer over the steel. Ichy began to pound on the door.

Kanji moved the blade to within inches of his belly. He could hear his father's words: "Samurai crackpot."

Ichy hurled his powerful body against the door, the sound shaking the altar in front of Kanji.

Kanji floated above the choice, the truth that had once faced his father.

A black ball ran rolling . . .

More words: A marathon is not life or death.

And still more: The only shame is a wrong death.

"Kanji! Kanji!" screamed Ichy as the door gave way.

Life. Death. Confusion. A black ball. Gleaming sword. Mosquitoes on his eyelids. Water cascading on his head. The eyes of Rai.

The warrior's sword fell from his hand.

Ichy rushed toward him, his eyes streaming with tears. He dropped down to his knees next to Kanji, searching for the blood from his belly.

"Life," Kanji said. "Life is the only value. My father was right."

Ichy picked up the sword, raised it above his gargoyle head and with one mighty blow slashed the Shinto altar into two pieces.

"I lost a race," Kanji said. "I will try again."

He would go back now, take the white dove from the monk's cupped hand, throw it to the sky and watch it soar into the sunlight, freeing himself.

* * *

Two hours in the recovery room, and Roy Holt was now in his hotel room, packing his suitcase.

Soldier Burns waited for him. He was going to take him to the hospital. Roy had requested it; he didn't want to take any chances after Oslo.

"You know what you did out there today?" Soldier asked.

"I'm not sure," Roy said.

"You put your feet smack on the runner's moon," Soldier said.

Maybe, thought Roy. He was not sure now. The great barrier, the folly of a single man, seemed already distant. For years he had wondered what he might feel at this moment. He knew now only that special peace of a man who had tried to be honest with his life and craft. He knew that this search had somehow defined him, that something had been tested and judged authentic within himself—and for those left out there who might have understood. He thought: Buck Lewis should be here. He would have the words. The Ulysses impulse? Human self-conception—without fear or limits. He could get on with his life now, for he was certain that he had found a thing that he could never lose, no matter what bad turns his future might take. He walked to the window and watched the last men and women drift in the dusk toward the finish of the Boston Marathon.